Dear Reader,

I just wanted to tell you how delighted I am that my publisher has decided to reprint so many of my earlier books. Some of them have not been available for a while, and amongst them there are titles that have often been requested.

I can't remember a time when I haven't written, although it was not until my daughter was born that I felt confident enough to attempt to get anything published. With my husband's encouragement, my first book was accepted, and since then there have been over 130 more.

Not that the thrill of having a book published gets any less. I still feel the same excitement when a new manuscript is accepted. But it's you, my readers, to whom I owe so much. Your support—and particularly your letters—give me so much pleasure.

I hope you enjoy this collection of some of my favourite novels.

Anne Mather

Back by Popular Demand

With a phenomenal one hundred and thirty books published by Mills & Boon, Anne Mather is one of the world's most popular romance authors. Mills & Boon are proud to bring back many of these highly sought-after novels in a special collector's edition.

ANNE MATHER: COLLECTOR'S EDITION

JAKE HOWARD'S WIFE

BY

ANNE MATHER

MILLS & BOON®

*First published in Great Britain 1973 by Mills & Boon Limited
This edition 1997
Harlequin Mills & Boon Limited,
Eton House, 18-24 Paradise Road, Richmond, Surrey TW9 1SR*

© Anne Mather 1973

ISBN 0 263 80550 6

*Set in Times Roman 11 on 12½ pt by
Rowland Phototypesetting Limited
Bury St Edmunds, Suffolk*

74-9709-45102

*Printed and bound in Spain
by Litografía Rosés S.A., Barcelona*

CHAPTER ONE

THE inter-city express was nearing King's Cross. It was running between the high tenement buildings that did not endear this section of the city to its planners. More contemporary were the soaring skyscrapers, as ugly in their way as the tenements; slabs of concrete and glass, stark and impersonal. At least the tenements had lines of grimy washing outside to advertise human habitation. The skyscraper flats could have been some kind of monolithic temples to the gods.

Jake Howard glanced up from the papers strewn on the table in front of him and registered his whereabouts with a faint flicker of surprise. London; only two and a half hours after leaving York. How easy it was to get about these days! He could have flown down, of course, but he enjoyed the train journey. It reminded him of his youth, of his first impressions of the big city, of the young, inexperienced fool he had been then.

A steward tapped on the window of his private compartment and with an imperative gesture Jake indicated that the man could enter.

'Only five minutes to King's Cross, Mr Howard,' he said, politely, deferentially. 'Is there anything else you need, sir? Another drink, perhaps?'

Jake shook his head, and sliding his hand into his trousers' pocket drew out a five-pound note. 'Nothing else, thank you,' he replied, handing the man the note. 'But you can arrange for the luggage to be taken to my car when we arrive.'

'Of course, sir. Thank you, sir. I hope you've had a pleasant journey.'

Jake's grey eyes narrowed ironically. 'Reasonably so, thank you,' he drawled.

The steward smiled politely and withdrew. After he had gone Jake began to thrust his scattered papers back into his briefcase. During the course of the journey he had been able to complete his assessment of the Havilland deal and he felt confident that there would be no hitches there. Havilland Chemicals would soon be part of the Howard Foundation, and that pleased him enormously. Of course, he would need to discuss the details with Sinclair in the morning, but that was merely a formality.

He finished putting his papers away, and taking out a case of cigars put one between his teeth. He lit it casually, resting his dark head against the soft upholstery. Outside the train's slightly misted windows the lights of the town glimmered brightly. It was after seven and it was too late in the year to expect the light to last much longer. It was cold, too. He had felt it as he waited for the train on the station at York; the sharp biting blast of an east wind accentuating the already cold October weather. After the heat of the west coast of the United States it was doubly chilling.

He smiled to himself. What a way to return to London from California; via Glasgow, and York railway station! But it was his usual practice. He always spent his first night back in England with his mother, and as she lived in Selby, in Yorkshire, he invariably flew into Prestwick and travelled south from there.

His thoughts moved on, over the irritating moments of changing from train to his chauffeur-driven limousine, to his eventual arrival at his own home, his house in an elegant square in Belgravia. And to Helen, his wife. . .

His lips twisted as he thought of Helen. By now she would have received the flowers he had despatched from Glasgow, and would no doubt be ready and waiting to greet him. He drew deeply on his cigar recalling the exquisite appointments of his house, anticipating with the pleasure of possession an evening spent in his wife's company, when he would regale her with the details of his trip.

And she would listen. Helen always listened, he thought disparagingly, and felt again the amazement he had felt three years ago when she had accepted his proposal and agreed to become his wife.

Then, of course, he had despised her. All his life he had had to strive to make his successful way in life. Born the son of a Yorkshire weaver, he had had to work hard to achieve any kind of position, spending all his days and nights, too, furthering his education, dragging himself up by his finger nails towards his goal. He would have gone to any lengths to succeed. He had a ready charm, and was quite prepared to use it to get what he wanted. He flattered and was pleasant to people he secretly found contemptible, he charmed people, men and women alike, and his innate intelligence was sufficient to guarantee him not to put a foot wrong. Unlike his father he was not interested in the mill; he was interested in chemicals. From an early age, he had found the study of substances and how they were formed fascinating, and a degree at Leeds University paved the way for greater things. He had the good fortune to get a job as laboratory assistant in a small chemical works near Selby, and although at the time his friends and relations thought he was a fool for confining his talents to such a small laboratory when he could have got a job with one of the larger concerns, Jake was already thinking ahead. By making himself indispensable to Mr Quarton, the works' managing director, and charming to Quarton's wife, it became a natural process for Quarton to take him on as a director of the firm. It was a short step from there to the chairman's position, and Jake was nothing if not persistent.

Now he tapped ash into the fitted tray and moved his shoulders wryly. He supposed he ought to feel some shame, some remorse at the way he had systematically gained control of Quartons and in so doing laid himself open for bigger bids. When the offer came he had no compunction about destroying the smaller firm in order to get a seat on the board of a larger company.

After that, it became easy, and in some ways less satisfying. He had been used to using his brain to its ultimate ability and even today, with his own foundation and more than a million pounds in stocks and shares, he refused to delegate duty.

Three years ago, when he met Helen, he had been on the lookout for a wife, a suitable wife, of course. There had been plenty of women on his rise to the top; office girls and models, the wives of some of his colleagues, all of whom had shown themselves more than willing to make themselves indispensable to him.

But in spite of the quantity, it was quality Jake was looking for. As in all things, only the best would do. And that was when he met Helen Forsythe.

He had known her father some years before, Gerard Forsythe, and had considered him a pleasant, if somewhat dilatory, member of the

London social set. Gerard's father had been
Sir Edwin Forsythe, Bart., of Mallins, near
Aylesbury, but unfortunately Gerard had been the
younger son and in consequence his brother had
inherited the title. But for all that Gerard Forsythe
had exactly the kind of background Jake would
have chosen had he had the chance. That Gerard
had squandered the money his father left him
meant little to Jake. In Gerard's position he knew
he could have made the money work for him, but
just because Gerard hadn't didn't alter his social
position.

However, when Gerard died, in a motor accident after a particularly bad evening at the card
tables, Helen was left almost penniless at only
twenty-three years of age.

She could have got a job, of course, Jake
realised that, but up until the time of her father's
accident and the subsequent scandal it engen-
dered, she had been practically engaged to Keith
Mannering, son of the barrister, Geoffrey
Mannering, and had spent her time enjoying herself. There had been skiing at St Moritz, and the
Bahamas in late autumn, and the usual London
social season to fill her days, and the idea of any
other kind of life had not crossed her mind. But
when her father was killed and Keith became
rather elusive she was left high and dry, with
only a small private income, inherited from her
maternal grandmother, to live on. She had been

well educated, had spent two years at a finishing school in Switzerland, and could speak several languages fluently. But apart from organising dinner parties and entertaining her father's guests she had never had to work in her life.

Jake had met her quite by accident at the Shaftesbury Theatre. He and some friends had been having a drink in the bar during the interval when Helen came in with a notable young married couple. Helen had been at school with the wife, and almost out of compassion for her they had invited her to join them for the evening. And as the husband was Giles St John, a close friend and business associate of Jake's, it was natural that the two should be introduced.

Jake had been escorting a rather exotic young woman from the Portuguese Embassy that evening and he had thought Helen had looked rather coolly on the Portuguese girl's attempts to display her proprietorial claim on Jake. He could not imagine Helen, with her Scandinavian fair beauty, her tall, slim, young body, and cool blue eyes ever succumbing to such a display, and it was in that moment that the seed of his idea had been formed.

He knew of Helen's situation, of course. It was common knowledge among the set he moved in, and he thought he saw something like challenge in the cool gaze she cast in his direction. It was unusual for him, for women usually found his lean dark features attractive. But Helen Forsythe looked at him as if he was a particularly obnoxious species of animal brought in for her inspection, and for the first time in his life he was aware of his northern accent only lightly veneered with polish.

He had contacted her the following day and asked to see her again. She had refused, and thereafter for several weeks she did the same. And then one day he called, and he could tell from the tone of her voice over the telephone that something was wrong. She agreed to meet him for dinner that evening and over the meal he got it out of her that the house she was living in was going to have to be sold. It was too great a drain on her resources, and she was at her wits' end to know where to turn. Gerard had been ostracised by his own family for his irresponsible ways and she refused to consider contacting them. Jake listened to her pour out her troubles, offered advice and sympathy, and left it there.

He telephoned her every day for a fortnight, sometimes inviting her out, sometimes merely asking how she was. He began to be aware, by a subtle change in her attitude, that she was beginning to rely on those phone calls. So he stopped them, and for over a week he did not contact her at all. It was like a business deal. He used strategy; uncaring that in this instance he was dealing with a human being, not a company.

When he contacted her again she was desperate, and that was when he put his proposition to her. He was not attracted to her, she was too cold, too controlled to appeal to his sensual nature. But she was ideal for his purpose.

To begin with his proposal had staggered her. Although the idea of becoming his wife had apparently not occurred to her she did not appear to find the prospect entirely objectionable. But his terms of reference, as he phrased it, were. He explained quite coolly that he did not want a wife in anything but name. He wanted her as an elegant possession to grace his table, to entertain his guests when necessary, and to be a pleasing advertisement of his taste in women.

His proposal had one definite effect. It froze the thawing of her attitude towards him so that she became again the cool, aloof female he had first encountered in the Shaftesbury Theatre bar.

Of course she accepted, as he had known she would, and that was why he despised her. He would have regarded her much more favourably if she had refused him, if she had shown a bit of spunk and set to work to organise her affairs. In consequence, he saw her only as a helpless creature, prepared to accept a man she obviously disliked as her husband rather than dirty her hands.

His own mother had been horrified. His father had died during the years of his rise to success and although he had wanted to bring his mother to London to share his home she refused to leave the house where she had spent so many happy years with Jake's father. But in spite of the differences in their outlook, in their positions in society, Jake still regarded his mother as the most admirable woman he had ever met.

Helen met his mother at the wedding. It was a fashionable affair, paid for by Jake, of course, to which all Helen's erstwhile friends came to wish her well. Jake wondered whether Helen actually believed their excuses of polite regret at not having seen her for so long, or whether she would take up their eager invitations. He was well aware that by marrying him she was putting herself back into that privileged society where possessions counted for so much more than personality.

Jake's mother had been out of place at the wedding as he had known she would be, just as Helen was out of place with her. Mrs Howard had never been one to mince words and she made it painfully clear that she considered her son could have done much better. Her working-class morality revolted against this thing Jake was perpetrating, for even she could see that his emotions were in no way involved with this cool, haughty girl.

And yet, in spite of the incongruity of its beginnings, the arrangement had worked well for both of them. Jake's work took him abroad a lot and in the three years of their married life they had only spent about three months together. But for all that, Helen was there on those occasions when Jake needed her, and if their relationship had never progressed beyond the bounds of polite strangers, they were at least civil with one another, which was more than could be said for many of their acquaintances.

Jake had discovered that she had exquisite taste in furnishing and decoration, and his house in Belgravia had become quite a showplace. With an unlimited supply of money, Helen had allowed her talent free rein, and Jake was comfortably aware that his friends considered him a very lucky man to have such an accomplished as well as decorative wife.

The train was running into King's Cross now and Jake got to his feet and reached for his sheepskin coat. He put it on and then raked a careless hand through the thick darkness of his hair. He was a big man, tall and broad, yet he moved with the lithe feline grace of a panther. He was not handsome, no one could accuse him of that. His nose had been broken in fights at school and his forty years had carved lines of experience beside his mouth and eyes. Yet for all that, women seemed to find him very attractive, although he was not foolish enough to imagine that his material wealth did not add to the image.

The brakes ground into the iron wheels and the

big diesel engine brought its load to a screeching halt at the barrier. Jake picked up his briefcase and emerged into the corridor just as the steward appeared with his cases. Latimer, his chauffeur, was waiting on the platform and he touched his cap politely when he saw Jake.

'Good evening, sir. Had a good journey?'

'Fine, thank you, Latimer. Are you well? Your wife?'

It was the usual greeting, the usual small talk as they walked down the platform to where the big limousine was waiting for them. The steward carried the cases, and passed them over to Latimer as they reached the car.

Jake slid behind the wheel and waited, lighting another cigar, tapping his fingers impatiently against the steering wheel. Now that he was here in London he was impatient to be home. It was more than three months since he had left for the United States.

Latimer finished stowing the luggage in the boot and came round to climb into the passenger's seat. Jake always preferred to drive himself unless he had work to do. The big car moved smoothly away and Jake relaxed. The snarl-ups of traffic in the city were of little consequence after the boardroom tactics he had had to face in San Francisco, and it was a relief to put all that behind him and concentrate on more ordinary things.

'How is Mrs Howard, Latimer?' Jake changed

down rapidly and stood on his brakes as a brilliantly painted Mini shot across in front of him. 'Did she get my flowers?'

Latimer cleared his throat. 'Yes, sir, she got them. I believe she's very well, sir. I think everyone's had a taste of cold, though, since the weather changed.'

Jake nodded thoughtfully. 'And your family are okay? How is that son of yours doing? The one at university. Do you think he'll go in for physics and chemistry?'

'He wants to, sir.' Latimer sounded enthusiastic. 'His results are satisfying so far, I think. He's into his third year now, you know. I'm sure he appreciates your interest, sir.'

Jake's lips twisted a trifle ironically. He doubted whether Alan Latimer shared his father's attitude. Like all young people he was arrogant, and while he might be glad of a chance to work in the Howard Foundation laboratories, he certainly wouldn't beg for such a position. Jake admired his spunk. Alan was like he had been, eager to succeed and impatient of his father's dated ideas of one's station in life.

Jake's house stood in Kersland Square, a tall Georgian building with wrought-iron balcony rails and urns of flowering plants by the door. The door was painted white with a brass knocker, and it was one of a row of such houses all owned by business or professional people. Latimer, whose wife was also housekeeper in the establishment, and his family lived in the basement in a modern self-contained flat that was the envy of their friends and relations.

Jake stopped the limousine at the door and slid out.

'Will you be needing me any more this evening, sir?' Latimer had climbed out too and was standing awaiting instructions.

Jake turned up the collar of his coat against the cold night air. 'I don't think so, thanks,' he replied, shaking his head. 'You can put the car away.'

'Yes, sir.' Latimer saluted and Jake turned and mounted the steps to the front door, letting himself in with his key.

He stepped into a wide hallway, carpeted in shades of blue and gold, with pale oak-panelled walls and a crystal chandelier suspended overhead. It was a beautiful entrance, its only piece of furniture an exquisitely engraved oak chest on which was standing a vase of dahlias, their closely curled heads providing dashes of colour against the panelling.

To the right and left of the hall, panelled doors gave on to dining and reception areas, and Jake's study. But these doors were presently closed, and Jake frowned as he unbuttoned his coat, throwing his briefcase carelessly on to the polished surface of the chest. Where was Helen? She always came out to greet him. Hadn't she heard the car? Or the door being opened?

He threw off his coat and was about to cross the hall when the door at the back of the stairs which led to the kitchen and basement quarters opened and Mrs Latimer appeared.

She smiled warmly, and took his coat from him. 'Good evening, sir, and welcome home! Have you had a good trip?'

Jake forced himself to be polite. 'Fine, thanks, Mrs Latimer. How are you?' The question was perfunctory, and he glanced round impatiently.

Mrs Latimer answered quietly, her gentle face troubled. She was a small woman, with greying brown hair and a friendly countenance. She had been with Jake for the last ten years, since her youngest child was old enough to fend for itself, while her husband had worked for him for over thirteen years. They knew their employer very well by this time, and she sensed his intelligent query.

'Where is Mrs Howard?'

Mrs Latimer coloured. 'I'm afraid she's out, sir.'

The hell she is! Jake suppressed the angry outburst. 'Where?'

'I'm not sure, sir. She didn't say. I only know she's with Mr Mannering.'

'*Mannering?*' Jake was astonished. '*Keith* Mannering?'

'I believe so, sir.' Mrs Latimer looked uncomfortable. 'Er—I've dinner ready, sir. I expect you're hungry. If—if you'd like to wash—'

Jake loosened his tie. 'Tell me,' he interrupted her, his eyes distant, 'did my wife know I was expected home this evening?'

'Of course, sir. Your flowers arrived from Glasgow yesterday evening.'

'I see.' Jake narrowed his eyes, the feeling of homecoming, of complacency almost, which he had felt coming here in the car vanishing beneath a tide of fierce resentment. 'Very well, Mrs Latimer. I'll take a shower. I'll eat in'—he consulted the broad gold watch on his wrist—'in say twenty minutes.'

'Yes, sir.' Mrs Latimer nodded politely, and without another word Jake went up the stairs, taking them two at a time, his temper simmering.

He thrust open the door of his bedroom and entered the room, kicking the door to behind him. It was an attractive room, chocolate brown walls and an apricot bedspread toning well with light oak furniture and deeper apricot drapes. In the light of the lamp by his bed it should have soothed him, but it didn't. He felt furiously angry, betrayed almost, that Helen should choose this evening of all evenings to be out. She had never done this before. She had always been there when he arrived back from one of his business trips, ready to smile and listen to him as he told her of his dealings, ready to offer sympathy or tentative advice if required. Goddammit, he thought violently, that was what she was here for. He had *bought* her for that purpose, not to go gallivanting off with bloody Keith Mannering!

He stripped off his clothes and walked naked into the bathroom, turning on the shower and stepping under it, uncaring that he soaked his hair. He moved beneath the sensuous stream of water, enjoying its cooling balm to his heightened senses. How dared she be out? he thought furiously. How dared she allow her name to be coupled with a man who had deserted her three years ago while he, Jake, was out of the country? God, what would his friends be saying? What would they be thinking?

He turned off the shower and wrapped a huge bath-sheet about him, towelling himself dry automatically. Then he rubbed his hair thoroughly and went back into his bedroom. He dressed in closefitting black suede trousers that moulded the strong muscles of his legs, and a cream silk shirt. He didn't bother to dress formally. There was no point. And besides, he was in no mood to put on a dinner jacket.

On impulse he crossed the landing and opened the door of Helen's bedroom. Switching on the lamps, he surveyed its feminine charm sardonically. There was a soft fluffy white carpet underfoot, while the bedcoverings and curtains matched each other in delicate shades of rose pink. The dressing table was strewn with jars and bottles and atomisers, the usual paraphernalia found on any woman's dressing table, while a sliver of chiffon lay carelessly at the foot of the bed where she had discarded it. Jake's teeth fastened harshly on his lower lip and he switched out the lamps abruptly and closed the door with a decisive click. He was amazed at the anger that was gripping him. He had the strongest impulse to do something quite violent. How dared she do this to him? he asked himself again, as he descended the thickly carpeted staircase. Who the hell did she think she was dealing with? Some blasted nondescript, who hadn't the sense he was born with? Some ignorant northerner who wouldn't object to his wife having aristocratic boy-friends? No, by God, not he, not Jacob Anthony Howard! When he acquired a possession it was his, in its entirety, not just part of the time, not just when he chose to take it out and look at it, but always!

He crossed the blue and gold hall and entered the low, light lounge that gave on to the dining area. The lounge was large and lit by concealed lighting along the ceiling moulding. It was decorated in shades of blue and green, and its soft, feather-cushioned sofa and armchairs were massive and extremely comfortable. It was a comfortable room, a lived-in room, vastly different in design from the reception lounge across the hall where he did most of his entertaining.

The dining area was divided from the lounge by a teak librenza, fitted with bookshelves and places for *objets d'art*. Helen collected articles in jade and ivory, and there were several exquisitely carved pieces on the librenza. The dining table was dark polished wood with some dark, leather-seated, ladderbacked chairs to match it. Mrs Latimer had laid a place at the table for him, the rush place-mat and silver cutlery reflected in its polished surface.

Jake regarded her ministrations silently for a moment or two and then with an impatient gesture he walked across to the cocktail cabinet and poured himself a stiff Scotch. He swallowed it at a gulp and poured himself another before flinging himself into one of the enormously soft arm-chairs, draping one leg over its arm.

He looked round the room restlessly, unable to relax. Nothing had changed. The turquoise velvet drapes at the windows toned marvelously with the soft blue-green of the carpet into which one's feet sank luxuriously; his hi-fi equipment in its polished teak cabinet still stood in one corner, while the unblinkingly broad screen of the colour television matched it in the other. Bookshelves flanked the marble fireplace in which an electric fire gave out a pseudo-log effect, unnecessary now that the powerful central heating system was in operation. The tasteful mixture of ancient and modern should have pleased him, but he found nothing to appreciate in it. He was consumed with resentment and anger, and it infuriated him that he should have arrived back here with such enthusiasm, only to have that enthusiasm doused by the thoughtless attitude of his wife.

Mrs Latimer appeared in the aperture which led to the dining area. 'If you're ready I'll serve dinner, sir,' she suggested politely.

Jake swung his leg to the floor and rose abruptly to his feet. 'Yes. Yes, all right, Mrs Latimer. I'm coming.'

He finished his drink and left his empty glass on the cabinet before crossing the room to the dining area. Seated at the empty table, he tried to show interest in the food his housekeeper had prepared. He was tempted to question her about Helen's activities while he was away. He wanted to know how often she had seen Mannering and whether he had been to the house. His jaw tightened. The idea of Keith Mannering here, in *his* house, was almost too much to contemplate without violence.

But he said nothing and attempted to behave as though Helen's absence was not important. Mrs Latimer had prepared his favourite dinner, roast beef and Yorkshire pudding with a raspberry crumble to follow, and he could not disappoint her by refusing it; although he might have been eating sawdust for all the enjoyment he took from it. He drank wine with the meal, a red Bordeaux that helped the food down. Afterwards, he carried his coffee into the lounge and after dismissing Mrs Latimer he switched on the television.

He seldom watched television. When he was home, which was not often, he was invariably entertaining or being entertained, and on those evenings when he might have relaxed he brought work home from the office and retired to his study to concentrate in its quiet luxury.

But right now he was in no mood to work; to study the contracts he had planned to study this evening after dinner, after he had discussed the merits of his trip with Helen. He was impatient for her to return home, to confront her with his anger, to make it plain once and for all that as his wife she had a certain position to uphold and no matter how unsatisfying their relationship might be she had chosen it, and by God, she was going to honour it!

Unwillingly, he recalled the young woman he had seen so frequently during the last few weeks. Louise Corelli had certainly helped to make his stay in California more enjoyable, but that was quite different, he consoled his conscience. He was a man, after all, with a man's appetites, and out of the country, thousands of miles from home and friends, from anyone who might gossip about their association. Helen was here, in London, where every move she made was speculated upon by friends and enemies alike.

The evening passed incredibly slowly and Jake's temper mounted to simmer somewhere around boiling point. He had turned off a particularly nauseating interview on the television and was in the process of pouring himself another Scotch when he heard Helen's key in the lock.

His first instinct was to march out into the hall and demand an explanation like some Victorian father, but he was too well versed in the arts of political tactics to waste his energy so carelessly. So instead he finished pouring his Scotch, swallowed half of it at a gulp and carried the rest with him to stand before the marble fireplace, one foot upraised to rest on the polished brass fender.

Helen must have seen the light, for a few moments later after she had shed her wrap, the lounge door opened and she stood on the threshold looking at him, her eyes slightly wary, he thought.

It crossed his mind with clinical detachment that she was looking particularly beautiful this evening. Her gown was a caftan of peacock blue embroidered with silver dragons which he had brought her back from Japan six months ago. Its severe lines hinted at the swell of her breasts, the curve of her hips, the slender length of her legs. To his knowledge she had never worn it before and it annoyed him intensely that she should have put it on for Keith Mannering's benefit. The long lovely length of silver hair had been coiled into a Grecian knot on top of her head, while tendrils escaped at her ears to caress her cheeks and the nape of her neck. Hoops of beaten gold hung from her ears, the present he had bought for their last anniversary.

Jake allowed her gaze to fall before the penetration of his and she moved into the room with obvious reluctance. 'Hello, Jake,' she said, putting her sequinned evening bag on a side table with unnecessary care. 'You're looking well. Have you had a good trip?'

Jake controlled the angry retort that sprang to his lips. 'It was reasonably successful, yes,' he responded expressionlessly.

'Oh! Good.' Helen was forced to look at him again, and he saw the troubled expression in her eyes. 'I—er—I'm sorry I couldn't be here when you got back. I—I had an appointment.'

'So I heard,' he said, swallowing the remainder of his Scotch.

Helen coloured. 'Yes, well, I'm sure Mrs Latimer provided you with an excellent dinner—'

'To hell with Mrs Latimer!' Jake's anger exploded.

Helen clenched her hands together. 'Please, Jake—'

'Please be damned!' Jake tossed the exquisitely

delicate whisky glass in his hand. 'Where the hell do you think you've been?'

Helen swallowed with apparent difficulty. 'Mrs Latimer must have told you—'

'I'm not interested in what Mrs Latimer said!' snapped Jake. 'I want to know where you've been and with whom?'

Helen made a helpless gesture. 'I've been to a party—with Keith Mannering.'

Jake uttered an ugly expletive and Helen winced at his language. 'You bitch!' he swore angrily. 'I don't know how you have the nerve to stand there and tell me you've been out with another man, let alone *Mannering*!'

Helen squared her shoulders with an effort. 'Why not?' she asked succinctly.

Jake narrowed his eyes, thrusting his empty glass on to the mantelshelf. 'Why not?' he demanded fiercely. 'What do you mean, why not? You're my wife; that should be answer enough!'

Helen toyed with the exquisite diamond ring which Jake had bought her on their engagement; her eyes were guarded and he suddenly wondered what she was thinking.

'And you?' she said quietly. 'Is that answer enough for you too? That you're my husband?'

Jake's expression was grim. 'What the hell do you mean by that?'

Helen raised her dark eyebrows. 'I should have thought it was obvious. Do you think I am allowed to remain unaware of your conquests? Do you think I'm not constantly being sickened by so-called well-meaning confidences?'

Jake raked a hand through his thick hair. 'My God!' he muttered violently, turning away to stare unseeingly into the electric flames. 'And you think my—actions—entitle you to act likewise, is that it?'

'*No!*' The brief remonstrance was sufficient to cause him to swing round and face her again. 'No,' she repeated heatedly. 'I'm not like you! I'm not an animal giving in to every physical need of its body—'

'And I am?' His tone was ominous.

Helen flushed scarlet. 'I honestly don't care what you are,' she retorted, biting her lips. 'But I can see no grounds for you to complain about my behaviour. So far as I'm concerned, these last three months have been the last straw! I see no reason for me to cut myself off from my friends just because I'm married to you—'

'Might I remind you that your so-called friends soon deserted you after your father's accident?' observed Jake cuttingly.

Helen winced as though he had struck her. 'That's a rotten thing to say!' she burst out tremulously.

Jake shrugged his broad shoulders, surveying her appraisingly. It was the first time he had seen her so animated. Normally he was unable to arouse more than a flicker of emotion in her controlled features.

'But true, nevertheless,' he remarked now, his eyes never wavering from her face. 'Now what are you going to tell me? That I'm uncouth and a cad for mentioning such a thing? That I haven't the manners of that priggish lout, Mannering?'

Helen allowed her long lashes to veil her eyes. 'Keith is a gentleman,' she replied tersely.

Jake uttered a contemptuous snort. 'Oh, he is? And what is your definition of a gentleman, I wonder? Someone who never eats peas with his knife? Or maybe someone who only makes love in his pyjamas, never in the raw!'

Helen took a deep breath. 'You're crude!' she exclaimed distastefully. 'I'm going to bed.'

Jake crossed the room to her side in an instant, moving swiftly and lithely for such a big man. 'Oh, are you?' His mouth tightened. 'You'll go to bed when I say and not before.'

Helen lifted her head incredulously. 'Really, Jake, this is the twentieth century. You're not my keeper! You can't *make* me do what you want all the time.'

'Can't I?' His lips twisted. 'I shouldn't bank on that if I were you.'

Helen moved towards the door, but he was in her path. 'I don't like this conversation, Jake. I wish it had never taken place.'

'So do I!' he snapped sharply. 'Might I remind

you that your absence here this evening was
responsible.'

Helen sighed. 'I'm tired. Can't we discuss this
in the morning? We'll both be more—well—
reasonable, then.'

'What is that supposed to mean?' Jake glared
at her.

Helen made a helpless gesture towards the
glass on the mantelpiece and then seemed to
regret the impulse. 'It doesn't mean anything,'
she denied uncomfortably.

'You think I'm drunk, is that it?' Jake made a
derisive grimace. 'Dear God, you've never seen
me drunk, Helen!'

'Nor should I want to.' Helen quivered. 'Am
I to be allowed to go to bed?'

Jake stepped aside abruptly, but his jaw was
taut. 'Aren't you interested in what I've brought
you back from the States? I thought that was why
you married me—to retain the material benefits
of life!'

Helen looked as though she would have liked
to have struck his sardonic face, but she did nothing except clench her fists. Then she walked
out of the lounge, across the blue and gold
hall with its crystal chandelier casting prisms
of light on her pale hair, and up the stairs to
her room.

Jake watched her go with impotent fury and
then walked back into the lounge, slamming the

door behind him. When he finally sought his bed
the newly opened bottle of Scotch was three parts
gone. . .

CHAPTER TWO

HELEN applied a pale green eyeshadow to her lids, aware of an unusual feeling of apprehension when she considered the evening ahead. They were going to a reception at the embassy of one of the newly developing African states and it would be the first evening they had spent together since Jake's return from the United States almost a week ago.

He had been fully occupied since his return, she knew that from the long hours the lights burned in his study, but even so it had been a strange and uncomfortable week when their attitudes towards one another had undergone a subtle change.

Before Jake's trip to America they had talked quite a lot, mostly about business, she had to admit, but their relationship had never been strained as it was now. And it was all her fault. Or was it?

She dropped the applicator she had been using impatiently and studied her reflection critically in the mirror of the dressing table. Surely it was unreasonable of Jake to expect her to abandon people she had known since she was a child in favour of his associates and their wives. Granted some of his associates, Giles St John, for example, were friends of hers, too, but there were others, people Jake despised because of their attitudes, whom she found perfectly acceptable.

She looked round for the mascara and began to stroke it on to her already dark lashes. Keith Mannering came into this latter category. She had known Keith for years, and once she had expected to marry him. But that was all in the past now. Now they were just good friends, and it was contemptible that Jake should attempt to suggest otherwise.

She smoothed a colourless lustre over her lips, a look of strain momentarily touching the wide beauty of her green eyes. How often in the past had she had to suffer the ignominy of a purportedly well-meaning confidant feeling it her duty to let Helen know that some other woman was seeing Jake regularly? At first it had shocked and humiliated her, but eventually she had had to accept that there was nothing she could do about it. Jake was a sensual man and there would always be some women more than willing to satisfy his male appetites. She knew these women meant nothing to him, and as soon as they attempted to make demands upon him over and above what he had to give, he dismissed them from his mind without a second thought. He could be completely ruthless, and Helen could almost find it in her heart to pity them.

She arose from her position in front of the dressing table observing her reflection almost detachedly. The long white lace negligé revealed the slim yet rounded curves of her body, the slender length of her legs. She knew without any sense of false modesty that she was beautiful; Jake would not have married her otherwise. Everything he possessed had to be the best, but the knowledge gave her no pleasure.

With a sigh she reached for the fragile items of underwear strewn on the bed and smoothed sheer tights over her thighs. Her dress was a simple, yet elegant, tunic of black silk, secured about the waist with a tasselled cord. It accentuated the lines of her breast, dipping in front to reveal the creamy skin of her throat.

She was fastening diamond pendants to her ears when there was a distinct rap at her door and stiffening, she called: 'Come in!'

The door opened and Helen, viewing it through the mirror of the dressing table, saw Jake enter the room looking darkly attractive in his evening clothes. Even in such formal attire there was something entirely primitive about him, about the way he moved, the arrogant, ironic gleam in his dark eyes. He looked superbly confident and aware, and Helen realised that he was anticipating the evening ahead with a great deal of enjoyment. For him it was a challenge, an opportunity to use his innate talent for influencing people, and she knew he saw this reception as a step towards the Howard Foundation gaining a foothold in black Africa. Already he had laboratories in South Africa and Rhodesia, and the foundation's preparations were used throughout the continent.

But it was the man himself that emanated the enthusiasm that had built his empire, and no matter how powerful he became he would always have this driving ambition and compelling personality.

Helen revolted against this knowledge; she always had. She still didn't really know how ever she had accepted his proposal of marriage and placed herself in this enviable, and yet impossible, position of being Jake Howard's wife. His ruthless, calculating nature, his easy subduing charm, his complete confidence in his own ability; all these things repelled her, but she knew that was how it had to be. If ever she allowed him to get under her skin, it would be a devastating experience, and one she never allowed herself to contemplate.

Now he surveyed her appearance with almost insolent appraisal, his eyes narrowing at the challenge in hers. 'You look—beautiful,' he said, with consideration in his voice. 'But I'm sure you know that already.'

Helen allowed a little of the tension to slide out of her. 'It's always pleasant to have one's opinion reinforced,' she remarked smoothly, fingering a soft curl of silk which fell over one shoulder. She had secured her hair with a jewelled clasp on the crown of her head and only several casually deliberate strands caressed her cheeks.

Jake inclined his head sardonically and then produced a cream box from his pocket. 'I have a present for you,' he said, opening the lid. 'Do you like it?'

He extended his hand and Helen looked down at the brilliance of the necklace that lay on its dark blue velvet bed. Its setting was platinum, a looped fragile strand of diamonds and emeralds and rubies. Its beauty caught her breath but her expression remained composed.

'Thank you,' she acknowledged its acceptance with a faint smile. 'Will you put it on for me?'

Jake dropped the box on to her bed. 'Of course,' he agreed, his manner equally cool as he looped the necklace about her throat and fastened it with swift, expert fingers. 'There you are. I think it complements what you're wearing, don't you?'

Helen touched the coldness of the stones with tentative fingers. Against her flesh it had an added sparkle, gathering warmth from the creamy skin of her throat. Her fingers fell away to link together at her waist and she turned away from the mirror. 'Yes. It's exquisite,' she said expressionlessly.

Jake regarded her for a long compelling moment as though trying to gauge her real reactions to his gift and then shrugged his broad shoulders. 'I bought it in New York. I thought you would like it.'

'I do.' Helen bent to pick up her evening bag. 'Are you ready to leave?'

Jake lifted a mink stole that was draped casually across the foot of the bed and allowed Helen to move into it. 'Yes, I'm ready,' he affirmed, allowing the fur to fall from his hands. 'Latimer is just getting the car. Do you need a drink first?'

Helen flicked a glance in his direction. 'Do you?'

'I already have.' A faintly ironic gleam appeared in Jake's eyes. 'Your service, I believe.'

Helen did not allow him to see how his mocking sarcasm could annoy her. Instead, she walked towards the door and he had perforce to follow her.

Downstairs Latimer waited patiently in the well of the hall. He bade his mistress good evening and held open the door for both her and Jake as they left the house. Latimer was driving this evening. It was more convenient for Jake at affairs like these where there was always an abundance of food and alcohol.

The Embassy stood in a square off Bond Street and by the time they arrived there was already a steady stream of people climbing the shallow steps to the front doors. There was no room to park in front of the building, so Latimer was to take the car home and return for them later.

Jake helped Helen out of the car and said a few words to Latimer before turning and cupping her elbow as they mounted the steps together. They entered a wide marble hall where uniformed personnel were employed to direct guests to the cloakroom and Helen left Jake for a while to check in her stole and assure herself that her make-up was still as faultless as when they left home. The cloakroom was filled to capacity with women of all colours and nationalities, in all types of national dress; from the sleek sophistication of the cheongsam to the undoubted elegance of the sari, and Helen had only a hasty glimpse of her reflection before turning and emerging again into the entrance hall.

Jake was waiting for her, but he was not alone. A middle-aged man with a bristling moustache was talking animatedly to him while Giles St John and his wife Jennifer were standing close by listening. Jennifer waved energetically when she saw Helen and Helen walked towards them with enthusiasm.

'Helen, *darling*!' Jennifer kissed her cheek warmly. 'It's simply ages since we've seen you. What have you been doing with yourself?'

Jake's eyes strayed to his wife's slightly flushed face and Helen was intensely conscious of that look. She knew Jake was perfectly capable of appearing to give all his attention to one matter while he was actually listening to something entirely different, and she sensed his interest in her reply. Perhaps he expected her to tell Jennifer about seeing Keith Mannering.

So she smiled in her usual self-possessed manner, and said: 'I expect you've been busy. I know I have. And with Jake just getting back from the States. . .' She allowed the sentence to tail away in a smiling, deprecatory gesture and Giles took her attention.

'You're looking particularly extravagant this evening, my love,' he remarked teasingly, holding on to her hand rather longer than was necessary. 'Where did you get this particular bauble?' He touched the necklace at her throat with a light hand. 'I guarantee that wasn't bought at Woolworths!'

Jake had finished talking to the middle-aged politician by this time and he turned to listen to what was being said with smiling amusement.

'You think not?' he queried, in reply to Giles' comment, his eyes holding Jennifer's for a deliberately long moment, arousing a fluttering awareness inside her which Helen was instantly conscious of. Then he looked at his wife and his eyes narrowed perceptibly. 'One tries to improve upon perfection,' he observed dryly, and Helen felt the colour in her cheeks deepen annoyingly.

'I think this conversation is rather ridiculous, don't you?' she asked of Jennifer quickly. 'Oh,

Giles, did you find anything out about that *vin-aigrette*?' As well as being on the board of several companies Giles was an amateur enthusiast of the world of antiques and Helen had given him a small silver container which Jake had given her for her birthday which was reputed to have belonged to Lady Hamilton herself.

Giles went on to explain that he was still in the process of investigating it, and by mutual consent they moved towards the stairs, Helen walking with Giles ahead of the others. She could vaguely hear Jake relating some outrageously funny anecdote of his trip to the States to Jennifer and she was laughing excitedly. Helen's lips tightened almost imperceptibly. On the rare occasions when she had been depressed enough to complain about her husband to her friend, Jennifer had always sided with her in agreeing that Jake treated her abominably and that she personally found him despicable. And yet whenever they were all together Jennifer behaved as though she found Jake immensely attractive, and for the first time tonight it irritated Helen. She glanced round at them impatiently, a little of her annoyance showing in her face. Jake caught the look, however, and held her gaze for a long disturbing moment. Then Jennifer stumbled, whether by accident or design Helen could not be certain, and caught his arm, and his attention was distracted.

Helen continued up the stairs, but there was an

awful shaken feeling gripping her stomach. Jake had not discussed his American trip with her, indeed they had spoken little since his return, and it was infuriating that this knowledge upset her so. When Giles tugged a strand of her hair to attract her attention she turned to him with more enthusiasm than was usual, dazzling him with the brilliance of her smile. She was allowing the whole affair more importance than it demanded and she closed her ears to Jennifer's whispered confidences. Giles didn't appear to notice, so why did she?

The reception lounges at the top of the stairs were filled with people, all talking and laughing and helping themselves to the liberal supply of alcohol, and a major-domo in formal dress announced their names as they entered. One of the Ambassador's aides greeted them politely and introduced them to several other officials, and then someone else was arriving and they were left to mingle.

Helen saw Jake looking about him with interest over the rim of his whisky glass and she sipped her champagne cocktail a little resignedly. She knew that look. It was the predatory look of the tiger when it is getting ready to pounce, and she knew that for the moment Jake's mind was occupied with business. As though to illustrate this point, Jake excused himself from them at that moment on the pretext of speaking to some politician he knew and he disappeared among the crowd almost before anyone had time to voice an objection. Jennifer looked almost pityingly at her friend, and said wryly:

'I suppose that's the last we can expect to see of your husband for an hour or two. Really, he is the absolute limit, don't you think?'

Helen bent her head, stroking the rim of her glass with an absent finger. 'I suppose so,' she conceded quietly.

Giles tucked an arm through each of theirs. 'I should care,' he remarked smilingly. 'At least he's left me with the two most attractive women in the room!'

Helen smiled, and Jennifer gave him a bored wrinkle of her nose. 'But what are we expected to do, darling? I mean—don't you know anyone of interest?'

Giles frowned and looked about him with concentrated attention. 'Well, I know President Lbari, over there with his wife. He was at Cambridge with me. His wife's a sweet girl. Used to be a nurse, I believe.'

Jennifer looked bored. 'Who is that man who is staring at us? That middle-aged man, over there. Do you know him?'

Giles flicked his gaze round. 'Oh, you mean Bertie Mallard. Yes,' he nodded his head in acknowledgement of the other man's raised hand. 'He's Lord Mallard, actually. You've heard me mention him, I'm sure, Jennifer. He's quite an expert on old furniture.'

Jennifer raised her eyes skyward. 'Heavens!' she remarked dryly. 'The excitement of that statement! Don't any *interesting* people come to these receptions, any *young* people?'

'Of course.' Giles finished his champagne. 'Come along. We'll wander round. You never know who we may come up with!'

Helen had, perforce, to accompany them, but deep inside she felt frustrated. Jennifer was right. Jake was the absolute limit. Why did he bring her to these affairs if he intended to abandon her?

They wandered round for fully an hour without coming upon Jake and Helen was accepting her fourth glass of champagne when a lazy hand trailed down her arm and she swung round to confront Keith Mannering.

'Keith!' she exclaimed, in surprise. 'What are you doing here?'

Jennifer and Giles turned too. Giles knew Keith quite well and they greeted one another with casual ease. But Jennifer gave him an extravagant smile.

'Keith darling!' she cried in her usual effusive manner. 'How marvellous to see you! I'm sure Helen's delighted, too. Her husband has deserted her and we're all feeling rather sorry for ourselves, aren't we, my pet?'

Helen gave Jennifer a hard stare. The very last

thing she wanted was for Keith Mannering to get the wrong idea. She liked him, they were friends, but that was as far as it went.

Not that Keith wasn't a very personable young man; he was. A little older than Helen, tall and slim and boyish, with smooth fair hair falling in a wave across his forehead, he had caused a flutter in several feminine hearts, and Helen was not unaware of this.

Now he smiled into Helen's eyes, and said: 'Actually I did come to see Helen, Jennifer. I managed to get tickets for that Mahler concert you wanted to hear and I wondered if we could arrange something.'

Helen made an expressive gesture. 'Oh! Oh, I see. I'm afraid I don't know, Keith. I mean— when we discussed the concert, Jake was still in the States. Now—well—he's home and it's rather awkward.'

Jennifer had listened to Helen's excuses impatiently, and now she exclaimed: 'Heavens, Helen, do you think Jake would consider you if there was somewhere he wanted to go? For goodness' sake, he's not your keeper. Make a stand! Be independent! Have your own friends. He has his!'

Helen pressed her lips together. She knew Jennifer was right again. Witness this evening, for example; she hadn't seen him since their arrival. It had been left to Giles to entertain her.

'I don't know, Keith—' she was beginning when she saw him stiffen sharply and glancing round she saw her husband approaching them with a purposeful stride. He had the satisfied expression of the cat who has just stolen the cream, but his eyes hardened as they alighted on Keith Mannering, and ironic speculation took the place of complacency.

'Well, well,' he remarked casually, as he joined them, sliding possessive fingers round the soft flesh of Helen's upper arm, which Helen immediately resented. 'It's Mannering, isn't it? What's a clean-living young lawyer like you doing in a place like this?'

The insolence was evident in his tone even though what he said was not in itself insulting. But as Keith was not so tall as Jake or so broad, he was immediately at a disadvantage. However, Helen had to admire the way he straightened his shoulders and replied, quite calmly:

'Actually, Howard, I'm here to see your wife. I've got tickets for a concert she particularly wanted to attend.'

Helen's eyes flashed from Keith's flushed young countenance to the cool, dark features of her husband. It was apparent from the cruel tightening of the hard fingers against her arm that Keith's instant explanation had surprised Jake, but he was never disconcerted for long.

'I see,' he said now, accepting a cigarette from

Giles, who had obviously chosen this moment to offer it in an effort to avoid the possible confrontation that was to follow. 'And why should you imagine I might not be taking my wife to this concert myself if she particularly wants to go?'

Keith hesitated. 'I understand from Helen that classical music leaves you cold, Howard,' he stated distinctly, causing Jennifer to expel the breath she had been holding on a faint gasp.

'My wife says that, does she?' Jake bent his head and lit his cigarette from Giles' hastily proffered lighter, and went on: 'You must tell me what else my wife says, Mannering. I'd be interested to hear her assessment of my musical appreciation—'

'Jake, *please*!' Helen looked up at him imploringly.

'Please what?' Jake regarded her coldly.

'Please don't cause a scene!' quietly. 'I've—I've already told Keith I can't accept his invitation.'

'Why?' Jake's eyes were distant. 'Have I forbidden you to do so?'

'*No!*' Helen looked round almost desperately. 'Jake, I don't want to go.' She twisted her evening bag between her fingers, aware of Jennifer's calculating gaze and of Giles' more compassionate one. Keith himself was looking rather uncomfortable now and she guessed he was regretting creating this situation, but then he had not known

Jake would react as he had. He didn't know him like Giles did, like *she* did!

'But I insist,' Jake was saying immovably. 'After all, if your—if Mannering has gone to the trouble to get tickets, then it's the least you can do. When is this concert, by the way, Mannering?'

Keith thrust his hands into his trousers' pockets rather jerkily. 'On Thursday week,' he replied tautly. 'The twenty-third!'

Jake frowned. 'The twenty-third? Ah, yes, I remember now. There's a conference in Paris on the twenty-fourth, so I shall probably be away that evening. I'm sure Helen will be glad of your escort.'

Helen glared at him furiously, hating him for arranging her life for her so carelessly. Why was he doing it? He hadn't liked it when he found she was out with Keith the night he returned from his trip to the States, so why was he pushing her into his company now? It didn't make sense.

Jennifer heaved a rather regretful sigh then, and Giles looked slightly relieved at the peaceful outcome of the exchange. He suggested that they made a move towards the buffet tables and Keith took the opportunity to excuse himself with a casual comment to Helen that he would phone her later.

After he had gone an uneasy silence fell on the group and even when Helen was confronted with the mouth-watering array of food that had been provided she found it difficult to find any appetite. She was intensely conscious of Jake's displeasure, as they all were, and regardless of whether he had chosen to take the initiative in pushing his wife into Mannering's company or otherwise, his ill-humour was patently evident. He assumed a brooding silence, answering only in monosyllables if he was spoken to, and generally creating a tense atmosphere about them. Helen was glad when the Ambassador himself came to speak to them and Jake became more relaxed and talkative in his presence. But then Jake was always pleasant to business acquaintances and from his attitude Helen would have guessed that the Ambassador was making things easy for him by co-operating in whatever scheme he had in mind.

Eventually they left the reception rather earlier than planned, and Jake chose to take a taxi home rather than call out his chauffeur. Helen sat stiffly in her corner of the cab dreading the moment when they would arrive home and she would be alone with her husband.

Mrs Latimer had already gone down to her own apartment when they reached the house and Jake rang down to let Latimer know that he would not be needed any more that evening, while Helen walked nervously into the lounge.

In the subdued lighting everywhere looked

warm and comfortable, and Mrs Latimer had left
some sandwiches and a chicken salad on an
occasional table near the couch in case they were
hungry when they got back.

Helen shed her stole and bent to switch on the
coffee percolater. These ordinary arrangements,
these ordinary tasks, diverted her attention from
the slightly ominous atmosphere that Jake was
deliberately creating and she stood for a moment
schooling herself to remain calm. After all, she
had done nothing wrong, nothing to be ashamed
of, so why did she feel the guilty party?

Jake came through from making the telephone
call, raking a hand through the thickness of his
dark hair. He had loosened the jacket of his suit
and looked disturbingly handsome. Helen seated
herself with apparent coolness on the couch and
looking up, said:

'Do you want some coffee?'

Jake shook his head abruptly, walking across to
the cabinet and pouring himself a Scotch. Helen
glanced round surreptitiously, but he had his back
to her, and suppressing a sigh she poured herself
some black coffee, adding only a little sugar
before raising the cup to her lips. She had had
several champagne cocktails that evening and the
strong aromatic liquid was reviving. But she was
still on edge, she couldn't deny it, and she tried
to calm herself by mentally reassuring herself that

she was a match for any ignorant Yorkshireman any day.

But the trouble was, Jake was not ignorant, and she knew it, and having seen the way he could verbally annihilate his business associates she doubted her ability to better that ruthless streak in him should the need arise. The only person who seemed to hold any influence with Jake was a couple of hundred miles away in Selby, and Helen had no desire to appeal to her mother-in-law, who she was quite aware despised both her and her way of life.

Now Helen poured herself a second cup of coffee and Jake moved away from the cocktail cabinet to come and stand before the fireplace. Her fingers trembled as she dropped a lump of sugar into the coffee and she stirred it unnecessarily hard before placing the spoon in her saucer. She was avoiding looking at him. She was afraid of the penetration of those dark eyes, and she had no intention of allowing him to see that he could disturb her in this way. Until now she had coped quite adequately with the situation, but up till now, she reminded herself wryly, she had complied with his every request and had certainly never given him any cause to regard her as anything more than the woman he kept at his London house as a hostess when he entertained there. The fact that she wore his ring meant nothing more than lip-service paid to the social system of the country.

She cupped the fragile china container in her hands and inhaled the aroma of freshly ground coffee. By asserting her right to accept the friendship of another man she had unwittingly destroyed the barriers she had purposely erected as part of their marital structure.

Jake finished his Scotch and she could feel his eyes on her, probing the sensitive skin of her ears.

With admirable composure she replaced the cup in its saucer and rose to her feet, hoping that his silence was to be the only outward sign of his anger. But as she turned, he said harshly:

'Where do you think you're going?'

Helen put a hand to her temple. 'I'm tired, Jake. I'm going to bed.'

'You're always tired,' he accused her grimly. 'Particularly if there's something unpleasant to face!'

Helen took a deep breath. 'I don't see that there need be anything unpleasant said here,' she returned carefully. 'I haven't done anything to be ashamed of. I'm not a child, Jake, to be made aware of its shortcomings after an outing. If you're annoyed about that business with Keith then you have only yourself to blame!'

'Like hell I have! My God, Helen, you're bloody cool! What makes you think I'll take that from you?'

Helen expelled a faint sigh. 'Jake, don't you think you've humiliated me enough for one evening? I don't know what Giles and Jennifer must be thinking!'

'Don't you?' Jake raised his eyebrow contemptuously. 'But then you don't know your friends very well, do you? You only see them as surface people. You never look below the surface, for motivations.'

'What do you mean?' Helen was indignant.

'What I say. Poor old Giles will be wishing he could be half as rude as me and get away with it, and Jennifer will be despising him all the more for showing so little spunk!'

Helen lifted her head. 'Jennifer wouldn't think anything of the sort. She thinks you're coarse! She dislikes you just as much as I do.'

An unwilling smile touched Jake's lips at her heated words, but it was not a pleasant smile. 'Like hell she does!' he remarked succinctly. 'Don't you know that your friend Jennifer would give practically anything to be in your position?'

Helen stiffened. 'What does that mean?'

Jake dropped his glass on to the mantelshelf with a noisy clatter. 'It means, my aristocratic innocent, that so far as I'm concerned Jennifer is easy game, get me? I only have to snap my fingers—'

Helen's breathing was swift and jerky, her breasts rising and falling quickly beneath the soft

black material of her gown. 'You—you're despicable!' she told him, with repugnance. 'And I
don't believe you. Jennifer's not like that. I've
told you—she despises you!'

Jake stood before her, legs slightly apart,
regarding her with brooding impatience. 'Want
me to prove it?' he demanded coldly.

Helen looked up at him for a long moment and
then her eyes fell before the anger in his. 'Oh,
no, no, of course not.'

'Why?' Jake's eyes narrowed mockingly. 'Are
you afraid I might be proved right?'

Helen shook her head blindly. She didn't want
to think. She didn't want to remember that
moment earlier this evening, on the stairs, when
she had heard Jennifer laughing with Jake. Then
she would have been prepared to believe almost
anything. But it wasn't true, it couldn't be.
Jennifer was her friend. . .and yet. . .

She turned away, retrieving her evening bag
from its place on the couch. 'I'm going to bed,'
she said unsteadily. 'I don't want to talk about it
any more.'

Jake flexed his shoulder muscles tiredly. 'And
of course that ends this discussion,' he observed
derisively.

Helen moved towards the door. 'What more is
there to say? I just don't understand you at all.
You complain when I happen to be out the
evening you returned home from America, and

yet now you've practically forced me to go to the concert with Keith—'

Jake uttered an expletive. 'While I was in the States you went out with Mannering, didn't you? You didn't give a damn what people might be saying. Well, when it gets around that I arranged this meeting with Mannering it will douse some of the speculation about your relationship with him. No one makes a fool of Jake Howard and gets away with it, just remember that!'

Helen halted, turning to face him. 'What are you saying now?'

Jake lit a cheroot from the carved box on the mantel shelf. 'You're tired. I won't trouble you with the details.'

'Oh, *Jake*!' Helen stared at him tremulously, hating his mocking superiority.

'Go to bed, Helen. As you said—you don't understand me. But you will, believe me, you will!'

Helen turned abruptly away. She wanted to face him with his own shortcomings, with the frequent affairs he was reputed to be having, but she found it impossible. It would sound like jealousy, and until now such an emotion had never troubled her. But tonight, after that moment on the stairs, she found the idea of him making love to another woman vaguely distasteful. . .

CHAPTER THREE

THE restaurant was crowded at this hour of the morning, filled with expensively dressed women taking a break from shopping, all talking and laughing, exuding an atmosphere of casual elegance and exclusive perfume. It was a meeting place for most of the fashionable set and Helen sat at a corner table with Jennifer St John, idly sipping her coffee, her green eyes surveying the room almost cynically as she did so.

Jennifer was in the process of helping herself to a second cream cake, looking down critically at the trim lines of her figure.

'I really must try and curb this craving for sweet things,' she remarked complacently, digging her fork into the soft sponge. 'I should hate to get pleasantly plump. Today's fashions simply don't go well with ample proportions.'

'I shouldn't think there's much danger of that,' replied Helen kindly, turning her gaze to her friend. 'You look pretty slim to me.'

Jennifer raised her eyebrows. 'Yes, but how long will I stay that way if I continue to eat this kind of thing?' She sighed. 'Do you remember when we were at school? We could eat absolutely

pounds of fattening things and never turn a hair.
I wonder why you begin to pile on the inches as
you get older?'

Helen replaced her coffee cup in its saucer. 'I
imagine it's because one gets so little exercise
now compared to what we did at school. I recall
we used to play quite an energetic game of tennis,
not to mention hockey!'

'Oh, gosh, yes, hockey!' Jennifer grinned reminiscently. 'You were rather good, weren't you? I
was always afraid someone would mistake my
leg for the ball.'

Helen chuckled. Recalling their schooldays
like this was reassuring somehow. In those days
she and Jennifer had been very close. Surely
things should not have changed so much. They
were both married now, of course, but it wasn't
only that. So often nowadays they seemed to have
so little in common.

Conversation lapsed for a while and then
Jennifer said, quite out of the blue: 'How's Jake?'
with casual interest.

Helen lifted her coffee cup again. 'He's all
right, I imagine. Actually, he's away.'

'Away? Again?' Jennifer's derision was
evident.

Helen ran her finger round the rim of her cup.
'He's in the north of England,' she explained,
with reluctance. 'He's gone to the chemical complex at Lees Bay—in Northumberland.'

Jennifer listened intently. 'I see.' She studied Helen rather thoughtfully, and then said: 'What happened the other night? After the Embassy reception? Was he terribly annoyed about Keith turning up like that?'

There was an avid kind of curiosity in her eyes now and Helen was loath to satisfy her inquisitiveness. After what Jake had said about Jennifer, no matter how she might deny its logic to herself, she felt slightly wary of the other girl, and she wondered whether this had been Jake's intention. Divide and conquer? She shook her head and replaced her cup in the saucer. She was becoming fanciful. Jennifer was interested, that was all.

Now she considered carefully before she said with deliberation: 'How could he be annoyed when he arranged that I should go to the concert with Keith himself?'

Jennifer looked vaguely dissatisfied. 'You mean he wasn't annoyed?'

Helen sighed. 'I didn't say that exactly. I said he ought not to have been, as he arranged it.'

Jennifer extracted a slim gold cigarette case from her handbag and offered it to Helen, who refused. As she put one between her lips, she said impatiently: 'I think you allow him to get away with murder, I really do. I wouldn't let Giles dictate to me!'

Helen ran her tongue over her dry lips. 'Jake

doesn't dictate either. Our arrangement works very well, I think.'

'What? Him away all the time, and you twiddling your thumbs at home?' Jennifer snorted. 'Do you think I'd let Giles go to all those exciting places alone?' She drew deeply on her cigarette. 'I would not! I'd insist on going with him.'

'You're in a slightly different position from me,' remarked Helen quietly. 'You love Giles— and he loves you.'

Jennifer tapped ash into the tray, twisting her lips rather ironically. 'I'm not so sure that's true any more,' she said sharply. 'Oh, it was once. Our reasons for getting married were real enough, but it doesn't last, you know. Once the glamour of the honeymoon has worn off, what are you left with? A day-to-day existence with a man who imagines making love is something you do at night, and always in the dark!'

'Jennifer!' Helen was shocked and it showed in her voice. However unhappy her own life had been she had always thought Giles and Jennifer ideally suited, and for Jennifer to speak so callously seemed completely out of character.

Jennifer gave an impatient shrug of her shoulders. 'Honestly, Helen, don't look like that! It's not the end of the world! I haven't suddenly discovered how I feel. I've felt like this for years now. It's just now and then I feel like breaking out, and you just haven't been around on those other occasions when I've been foolish enough to speak my mind.'

'But—but why?' Helen couldn't understand. 'Heavens, you've got everything, Jennifer. A lovely home, your own car, plenty of money, a husband who loves you—'

'But I'm bored, Helen!' exclaimed Jennifer irritably, leaning across the table towards her. 'Bored! Can you understand that?'

Helen shook her head and lay back in her chair. 'You've been married five years, Jennifer. It's time you had a family—'

'Oh, how parochial can you get!' Jennifer made a gesture of disgust. 'A family! My God, do you think I want some screaming infant in the house? Do you think I want any more responsibilities than I already have?'

Helen bit her lip. 'I never dreamt you felt this way.'

'I don't—most of the time, anyway. Which is fortunate, don't you think?' Jennifer lay back in her chair, inhaling deeply. 'Shall we have some more coffee?'

'What?' Helen was absent. 'Oh—oh, yes, of course.' She leaned forward and took charge of the pot, pouring coffee into both cups. Then she managed a faint smile as she pushed Jennifer's cup towards her. 'However did we get into such a morbid discussion? I'm sure there are more pleasant subjects—'

'We were talking about your husband's short-comings!' observed Jennifer, in a brittle voice. 'Which even you must agree are many and varied!'

Helen flushed. Just occasionally Jennifer got under her skin, and this was one of those occasions. She wished she had not agreed to meet her for coffee. But the morning had stretched ahead of her aimlessly and she had been glad to get out of the house.

When she did not reply Jennifer heaved a sigh and said: 'What's wrong with you, Helen? You seem different somehow. You used not to be so touchy about Jake's affairs. What's wrong? Are you beginning to realise money isn't everything?'

'I never thought it was!' Helen denied hotly, and her nails bit into the palms of her hands in her lap.

Jennifer grimaced impatiently. 'Well, stop looking so shocked at everything I say. I'm feeling bitchy, and you just happen to be around, that's all.'

Helen sipped her coffee, trying to appear cool and composed. Unwillingly Jake's words about Jennifer were coming back to her, and she found herself looking at her friend in a different light. What if Jake was right? What if Jennifer was ripe for an affair? *With him?*

Helen's palms moistened. During the three years of their marriage, she should have become

inured to Jake's proclivities, but she had not. And
the idea of Jennifer being interested in him was
something about which she found it impossible
to speculate. Surely her feelings were not
unreasonable, even with their abnormal relationship? Surely Jennifer would never. . . But she was
presupposing something that might never happen.
Even so, she could never regard Jennifer in the
same way again. This morning's display had
destroyed something irreplaceable.

She sought about desperately in her mind for
something to say to break the uneasy silence that
had fallen between them. If she didn't say something soon Jennifer would begin to suspect that
there were other reasons why Helen found it so
impossible to talk about her husband today.

But fortunately at that moment another young
woman stopped by their table and greeted them
both familiarly. Mary Sullivan was the wife of a
Member of Parliament, and she joined them at
the table for a while discussing the weather and
the new autumn fashions. By the time she left it
was time for Helen to leave too, and she rose
almost eagerly to her feet.

As they walked to the door, Jennifer said casually: 'When does Jake expect to get back? I'd
like you both to come and dine with us before
Jake disappears on his travels again.'

Helen controlled the desire to say she didn't
know when Jake would be back, and replied:

'Thanks very much, Jennifer. I think he'll be home by the end of the week. It's only a flying visit to the plant.'

Jennifer drew on her suede gloves. 'Oh, that's good! Will Sunday evening be suitable, then?'

Helen pressed her lips together. 'I don't see why not, Jennifer. But can I ring you to confirm it?'

Jennifer studied Helen's cool countenance thoughtfully. 'You are all right, aren't you, Helen?' she asked suddenly. 'I mean—what I've said hasn't upset you, has it?'

Helen managed a smile. 'Of course not, Jennifer. I've—er—I've got a headache coming on. I think I'll go home and lie down for a while.'

Jennifer looked relieved. 'Yes, you do that. And don't forget to ring about Sunday.'

'I won't.'

Helen smiled again and the two girls parted on the steps of the restaurant. Jennifer hailed a cab and drove away waving, and then Helen turned and walked slowly along Oxford Street. It was after twelve and she had told Mrs Latimer she would have lunch at one but right now she didn't feel very hungry. The conversation with Jennifer had left a nasty taste in her mouth and she wondered if she was particularly dense. Why was it that Jake had seen in a comparatively short time what she had failed to see over a period of years? She had never considered herself naïve, and yet she had assumed that Jennifer's was a happy marriage. From time to time she had even envied her such a gentle and uncomplicated husband, although she had had the sense to realise that Giles' very qualities which she admired would have prevented him from liaising such a cold-blooded and deliberate union as Jake had contrived.

She turned into Park Lane and on impulse crossed the road and entered the park. The sun was endeavouring to break through the low-hanging clouds and although a cool wind was blowing it was invigorating. She enjoyed the tug of the wind through her hair. There was something clean and exhilarating about it, and she walked briskly across the grass, swinging her handbag.

She was allowing the situation far too much prominence in her thoughts, she decided at last. Just because her association with Jake had taken a more personal turn of late did not mean that anything had changed. It was simply the normal development of relationships and she simply could not expect to go through life without upheavals of some sort. She had chosen this kind of life, after all. It had not been forced upon her. When her father died—she refused to consider any possibility that he might have killed himself—she had had to choose, and the satisfaction she had gained from the effects of this marriage on her father's family had been more than adequate.

When she returned to the house in Kersland Square she was in a much more relaxed frame of mind, almost prepared to believe that she had been making a mountain out of a molehill. Even Mrs Latimer's rather annoyed remonstrances that lunch had been waiting over an hour failed to arouse more than a flicker of conscience, but she apologised charmingly, winning the older woman's reluctant sympathy.

'There was a call for you a little while ago, madam,' Mrs Latimer advised her, as Helen seated herself at the dining table and began to do full justice to the chilled fruit cocktail that began the meal. 'It was Mr Mannering.'

Helen put down her spoon and looked up. 'Mr Mannering?'

'Yes, madam.' Mrs Latimer folded her hands importantly.

'Did he say what he wanted?' Helen frowned, lifting her spoon again, but without her earlier enthusiasm.

Mrs Latimer shrugged. 'No, madam. He asked if you would call him back as soon as you came in.'

'I see.' Helen swallowed a mouthful of grape-fruit. What could Keith want now? Unless it was to arrange about the concert. But that was still a week away.

Sighing, she shook her head and continued with her meal. 'All right, thank you, Mrs Latimer,' she said, smiling faintly. 'I'll ring later.'

But the meal was spoiled and although it was delicious Helen had lost her appetite. After this morning's conversation with Jennifer she had no desire to see anyone, and if that was Keith's intention he was going to be disappointed.

She rang his apartment about five and caught him in. He sounded delighted to hear from her and after the preliminaries, he said: 'Jennifer tells me Jake is away at the moment. I wondered if you'd care to have dinner with me this evening.'

Helen sighed impatiently. Jennifer hadn't wasted much time, she thought cynically. If Keith had rung the house before she got back at lunchtime Jennifer must have contacted him immediately after leaving the restaurant. She felt a twinge of resentment that Jennifer should interfere in her affairs like this, and then squashed the idea. After all, Jennifer probably thought she would welcome the chance to see Keith again. She still had not accepted that what they had had over three years ago now was as dead as last night's fire.

'I'm sorry, Keith,' she said, putting the right amount of regret into her voice, 'but I hadn't planned on going out this evening.'

'All the more reason for you to change your mind,' remarked Keith forcefully. 'Look, Helen, there's this new place out at Henley. I thought we might have a meal there, that's all. We needn't be late in coming back if you don't want to be.'

Helen hesitated, the prospect of her proposed evening stretching ahead of her. Mrs Latimer would serve dinner about seven and then retire and she would be left to her own devices for several hours before she could contemplate bed. She wasn't sleeping awfully well and there was no point in trying to relax too early in the evening. Images of Jake suddenly flooded her mind. What was he likely to be doing this evening? Would he be spending the evening alone in his hotel suite? She very much doubted it. It was much more likely he would be entertaining his managers and executives at some northern night club until the early hours of the morning. . .

On impulse, she said: 'All right, Keith, I'll come. What time shall we go?'

Keith was delighted. 'Would seven be too early?' he suggested eagerly.

Helen considered the slim gold watch on her wrist. 'No—no, I don't think so,' she replied, mentally calculating how long it would take her to bathe and dress. 'No, that'll be fine, Keith. Will you pick me up here?'

'Of course. See you later, then.'

Keith rang off and Helen replaced her receiver not without a trace of reluctance. Now that she was committed she realised she had not really wanted to go out this evening, and if Keith had not phoned she would most likely have interested herself in the television, or perhaps in that book she had bought herself a few days ago. As it was, she had agreed to spend several hours in the company of a man who while proving an amusing companion could nevertheless present difficulties of a more personal nature. Keith, like Jennifer, could not entirely accept that their involvement with one another these days was vastly different from what it had been years ago.

She spent an hour relaxing in the bath and then dressed in a white blouse of Venetian lace and an ankle-length black velvet skirt. The blouse had full sleeves and a low round neckline, while the buttonthrough front of the skirt only fastened to just below the knee, leaving a tantalising length of slender leg to be glimpsed every time the opening parted. She put her hair up this evening, winding it into a coronet of plaiting which added maturity to her otherwise youthful air. She was ready when the doorbell rang and as she had already informed Mrs Latimer of her plans the housekeeper went to let Keith in.

He was in the lounge waiting for her when she came downstairs trailing a cape of silver sables, and his eyes widened appreciatively at the beautiful picture she made.

'Have you helped yourself to a drink?' Helen asked, draping her cape over the arm of a chair.

Keith smiled wryly. 'Actually, no. Your house-keeper doesn't give me the warmest of welcomes, and quite honestly I'd be afraid to touch anything in this house without permission for fear I'd be accused of stealing.'

Helen chuckled softly. 'I'm sure you're exaggerating, but never mind. What will you have now?'

Keith glanced round apprehensively. 'Well—' he began reluctantly. 'There's no chance of that husband of yours marching in on us, is there?' He sighed. 'I mean—I'd hate to come into contact with the tiger in his lair!'

Helen shook her head slightly impatiently. 'Now I know you're exaggerating,' she declared, walking towards the cocktail cabinet. 'Come on: what's it to be?'

Keith hesitated. 'Scotch would be fine,' he said, and felt in his pocket for his cigarettes. Helen refused to take one and he lit one for himself with hands which Helen noticed were not quite steady. The idea that he might actually find Jake alarming was almost laughable, and yet Helen realised she ought not to find it so. She had seen more pugnacious men than Keith Mannering brought down by the strength of Jake's personality. It was not so much what he said but his attitude when he said it that gave him such tremendous influence over his contemporaries.

The roadhouse Keith took her to was newly

opened and backed on to the river. It was excessively modern, all plate glass and Swedish wood, and while Helen found it very impressive she did not altogether like it. She preferred somewhere smaller, somewhere with character, that was not ostracised by the local population.

Even so, the food was good and the conversation stimulating. Keith could discuss plays and books and concerts that they had both seen and Helen was glad to share opinions with him. It was so long since she had discussed artistic subjects with anyone, for even had Jake lived at home most of the time he would not have found such things particularly interesting. In his ruthless climb to the top he had found little time to devote to the arts, and in consequence his tastes were rough and unformed. He only enjoyed what appealed to his sensual nature, dismissing anything that required a deeper search for significance, and just occasionally Helen found herself agreeing with him. But only occasionally. She refused to accept that all things worthwhile must offer of themselves before proving worthy of attention.

Keith drove her home soon after ten and parked the car outside the house. Turning sideways in his seat towards her, his arm along the back of hers, he said: 'Are you going to invite me in for coffee?'

Helen glanced at her watch. 'I don't think so,'

she said awkwardly. 'I mean—it is late, and Mrs Latimer will have left long ago.'

'I know.' Keith's lips twitched in amusement.

Helen sighed. 'Keith, don't go getting the wrong ideas about me. Just because I've been out with you a couple of times doesn't mean—'

'I know.' Keith interrupted her impatiently. 'I know, you're married! Well, so what? What difference does that make to us? Everyone knows—'

'I don't want to hear what everyone knows,' said Helen firmly, sliding out of the car. 'Thanks for dinner. Ring me about the concert next week.'

Keith compressed his lips. 'You won't change your mind?'

'About the concert? No, why should I?'

'I didn't mean the concert, actually, as I think you know,' remarked Keith dryly. 'Okay, Helen, goodnight!'

'Goodnight, Keith!'

Helen took out her key and inserted it in the lock as Keith drove away. The hall was in darkness and she switched on the lights before closing the door, her eyes flickering swiftly to the lounge and study doors, but there was no telltale line of light to indicate that Jake had arrived back unexpectedly early from his trip to Northumberland.

Shedding her cape, she walked through to the kitchen and found a note from Mrs Latimer advising her that she had left coffee and sandwiches in the lounge. Helen smiled wryly. Obviously Mrs Latimer had expected them to return here for supper. She frowned. It disturbed her a little. She didn't like the idea of Mrs Latimer speculating about her relationship with Keith. Jake was suspicious enough already. Was it possible that he had asked Mrs Latimer to take a note of her comings and goings and advise him on his return?

Helen turned abruptly and walked back into the lounge. That idea did not appeal at all. Surely Jake would not do such a thing? She saw the pile of freshly-cut sandwiches under their perspex lid. Obviously there was more than Mrs Latimer would have made for her alone. She sighed impatiently. Heavens, she thought angrily, she wasn't a child. If she wanted to have friends, why shouldn't she have friends? Why did there have to be ulterior motives behind every action? She and Keith had known one another for years, long before there had been any question of an emotional entanglement. So why should things be any different now?

She hunched her shoulders and sat down, switching on the percolator and watching the tiny bubble rise and burst against the glass lid. The evening had gone sour on her and she didn't know why. She glanced at her watch. A little after eleven. What would Jake be doing now? Where was he likely to be at this hour?

She reached for a cup and poured her coffee,

adding milk and sugar. Why was she asking herself such a question? she thought angrily. She
didn't care where he was. She never had. Or was
it perhaps truer to say that as she got to know
him better she began to speculate a little further
each day? When they first got married it had
been different somehow. Then she had still been
wrapped up in the cocoon of grief that had enveloped her at the time of her father's death. It had
been such a terrible time, such a terrible shock!
They had been so close, cut off as they had been
from relatives, and relying on one another for
close companionship. They had each had their
friends, of course, but her father had always
seemed so young, so charming, he had never
seemed out of place in her set. It was only when
he died that she realised how little anyone else
had meant in that strangely artificial existence
they had shared. Even Keith's defection had not
affected her as it might have done. She had had
to accept that that phase of her life was over and
another phase was beginning.

She didn't really know how long it had taken
her to recover completely. Jake's long absences
and his sudden returns were like punctuation
marks in her life, each period becoming a little
more real, a little more acceptable.

Gradually, she had begun to live again, devot-
ing herself to making her home as attractive as
she could, becoming the kind of wife she knew

Jake expected. But what she had not been prepared for was this widening of contact, this deepening of awareness, this penetration of the shell she had built around herself after her marriage and which she had imagined impregnable. She had not taken human nature into account when she had contemplated the future, and to suddenly find that she and Jake could react towards one another exactly like anyone else had been a revelation.

She finished her coffee and rising from her seat she walked idly across to where the teak cabinet of the hi-fi equipment was standing. Touching the oiled surface of the wood, she caught her lower lip between her teeth. To Jake, she was like this inanimate object, a possession, nothing more, and until now an unprotesting one.

She looked up and sighed. What had she to protest about? She was well fed, well dressed, capable of buying anything she wanted without even asking Jake's permission—what more could any girl ask?

And certainly their marriage was a constant cause of dissatisfaction to her father's brother, who had had no children himself and who knew that should Helen produce a son he would automatically inherit Mallins on her uncle's death.

Helen allowed a twisted smile to touch her lips. Only she knew how remote that possibility was. . .

CHAPTER FOUR

HELEN came awake with the distinct impression that someone was watching her, and as she lifted a lazy hand to smooth the thickness of her hair from her eyes she saw Jake framed in the doorway to her bedroom, leaning with casual indolence against the jamb. Dressed in a blue lounge suit, the dark shadow of a night's growth of beard on his chin, he looked disturbingly masculine, and Helen shivered beneath the silk covers, drawing them to her chin almost defensively.

His expression grew cynical at her involuntary reaction, and he straightened abruptly. 'Don't be alarmed!' he remarked disparagingly. 'I haven't driven overnight from Newcastle with lusting thoughts of you in my mind! But I am tired, bloody tired, and I wanted to speak to you before going to bed.'

Helen tried to gather her confused senses. 'Why—why do you want to speak to me?' she asked apprehensively.

Jake lifted his broad shoulders and then allowed them to fall in an indifferent gesture. 'We're going away for the weekend,' he advised her calmly. 'It was all arranged last night. I tried to ring you, but there was no reply during the evening. Were you out?'

Helen couldn't prevent the pink colour from invading her cheeks. Lying here like this, unable to move without revealing some previously guarded section of her anatomy, she felt at an awful disadvantage, and she wished she had the courage to get out of bed and pull on the enveloping gown which lay at the foot of the bed.

Jake stepped across the threshold suddenly, the velvet of her evening skirt lying carelessly on the chair where she had left it catching his eye. He lifted the skirt with critical appraisal and the lace blouse fell out of its folds.

'So you were out last night,' he observed dryly. 'Might one ask where?'

Helen heaved a sigh. 'You're not my keeper, you know, Jake!' she exclaimed.

'Am I not?' Jake's eyes narrowed unpleasantly. 'Then tell me—who is?'

Helen seethed. 'Will you please get out of my bedroom? I want to get out of bed.'

'Go ahead! I'm not stopping you.' Jake folded his arms and stood regarding her mockingly, feet apart, his dark eyes daring her to do as he suggested.

Helen rolled on to her stomach. 'I hate you, Jake Howard!' she bit out fiercely.

'Why? Because I've come back and spoiled things with friend Mannering? It was him you were out with last evening, wasn't it? Oh, don't bother to answer, I know. Mrs Latimer told me.'

Helen swung back on to the pillows. 'So you've got Mrs Latimer spying on me, have you? How despicable can you get?'

Jake's expression hardened. 'When I rang last evening and could get no reply, I was concerned. Nothing more. Naturally I rang Mrs Latimer to find out where you were. The phone could have been out of order, you could have been ill— anything!'

Helen's colour deepened. 'Even so—' she began defensively.

'Even so, nothing.' Jake's arms dropped to his sides. 'However, I do not intend to waste any time on Mannering at this moment. I can deal with him later.' His jaw tightened. 'I gather you're not interested where we're to spend the weekend.'

Helen's brows drew together. In this contretemps with Jake she had forgotten the reason why he was back sooner than expected. 'Of course I'm interested,' she said uncomfortably.

Jake moved to the bed and stood looking down at her with a strange look in his eyes. 'Are you?' he questioned thoughtfully. And then: 'Ndana has a weekend cottage. He and his wife have invited us to spend the weekend with them.'

'*Ndana?*' Helen echoed weakly. 'But—but isn't he—'

'The Tsabian Ambassador? Yes, of course.'

'Then it was he—who you were talking to at the reception the other evening.'

'That's right.' Jake flexed his shoulder muscles. 'Now do you understand how important it is?'

Helen put a hand to her temple. 'I—I think so. When do they expect us to arrive?'

'For supper this evening. I thought we'd leave about four.'

'I see.' Helen bit her lip. The prospect of a country weekend was not unpleasant, but she could have wished for more time to compose herself. Of late she had become too introspective and it would not do for Jake to suspect she was becoming discontented with her life.

But Jake mistook the doubtful look in her eyes for something else, and his brow darkened ominously. 'What's wrong?' he demanded heatedly. 'Have you made other arrangements with Mannering? Did you suppose I wouldn't be back before the beginning of next week?'

Helen quivered. 'I have made other arrangements, yes,' she began tentatively, about to tell him about Jennifer's invitation, but Jake did not wait to hear the rest of what she had to say. Instead, he bent down to her angrily, imprisoning her with a hand either side of her, his face harsh, his eyes cold and penetrating.

'I'm giving you fair warning, Helen!' he muttered violently. 'I will not take much more of this from you! I *own* you, physically at least, and if our arrangement is no longer satisfying to you, if you're beginning to crave a more physical relationship with a man, then *I* shall do something about it, do I make myself clear?'

Helen's lips parted. 'What do you mean?'

Jake straightened. 'Oh, I'm sure you understand me perfectly,' he said grimly.

'You—you disgust me!' Helen's breath came in short gasps.

'Do I? Do I just?' Jake's lips twisted. 'Why, you mercenary little bitch, I shouldn't overplay my hand if I were you!'

Helen uttered a shattered sob, and turning on to her arm buried her face in the pillow. She had never felt so humiliated in her life, and she could not bear to look at his lean dark face.

Jake took a step towards the door and then he halted and turning, caught the silk bedcovers and wrenching them from her unresisting fingers, dragged them to the foot of the bed, exposing her slender frame clad only in the sheer chiffon night-gown. Then he walked abruptly to the door and opening it, glanced back at her derisively.

'The sight of the naked female body is no novelty, Helen,' he remarked cruelly, and went out, slamming the door behind him.

By the time Helen found the strength to drag herself out of bed it was well into the morning and a neglected tray of toast and coffee which Mrs Latimer had provided lay on the table beside her. But she had not felt like eating and certainly the prospect of the weekend ahead was looming larger every minute.

Downstairs Mrs Latimer was preparing lunch and she tut-tutted when she saw Helen's untouched tray.

'Is something wrong, madam?' she asked anxiously.

Helen sighed and shook her head. 'No, I wasn't hungry, that's all, Mrs Latimer. Er—did Mr Howard say whether he was getting up for lunch?'

'Getting up, madam?' Mrs Latimer frowned. 'Mr Howard's not in bed. He went out shortly after breakfast.'

Helen felt a confused headache invading her temples. 'When—when was this?' she asked. 'I—I saw Mr Howard myself, about eight o'clock.'

'Yes, madam. Well, he had breakfast, and then he went out. As far as I know he's not coming back for lunch.'

'I see.' Helen felt particularly dense. 'I'm sorry. I must have misunderstood what he said. And—er—don't do anything much for me for lunch, Mrs Latimer. I—I'm just not feeling particularly like eating.'

Mrs Latimer looked at her rather doubtfully.

'Oh, and Mrs Howard—' she began uncomfortably.

Helen turned. 'Yes?'

'I—I hope I didn't do wrong in telling Mr Howard that you were out with Mr Mannering last evening.' Mrs Latimer flushed. 'He—well—he wanted to speak to you and I had to say something.'

Helen pressed her lips together. 'That's all right, Mrs Latimer. It's no secret,' she said, rather shortly.

Mrs Latimer breathed a sigh. 'If you say so, madam.'

Helen made an involuntary movement of her shoulders, and then turning walked out of the kitchen. In the lounge she hesitated by the cocktail cabinet, surveying its comprehensive contents thoughtfully. She had never felt like a drink in the morning before, but right now she felt she needed some kind of sustenance.

However, she turned away, pressing a hand to her stomach and lifting the day's papers scanned the headlines disinterestedly. Finally, she lounged into a chair and lit a cigarette, drawing deeply on the nicotine, trying to soothe her shattered nerves. She knew perfectly well she had not misunderstood Jake, he had intended going to bed, so where was he now, and why? Was this weekend with the Ndanas on or off?

Stubbing out the cigarette, she went into the

hall and lifting the telephone receiver dialled the number of the Howard Foundation Building in Holborn. Her fingers shook a little as she sought the numbers, but at last she heard it ringing at the other end.

The receptionist recognised her voice immediately, and said: 'Yes, Mrs Howard! What can I do for you?'

Helen ran her tongue over her dry lips. 'I'm trying to find my husband,' she said, infusing a light tone into her voice. 'Is he in the building, do you know?'

'I'm afraid not, Mrs Howard. He has been here, but I'm afraid he's gone now.'

'Oh—oh, thank you.' Helen hesitated. 'You don't happen to know where—'

But just as she was asking the question a key was inserted in the door and the heavy panelling swung inward and Jake himself came into the wide hallway.

'Oh, it's all right,' she said hastily. 'He's here now. Thank you.'

She replaced her receiver awkwardly and faced her husband uneasily. Jake was still wearing the blue suit, but he had shaved and changed his shirt, and apart from lines of fatigue around his eyes she would never have guessed he had spent the night driving down from Newcastle. He had a wonderful physique, probably due to the fact that he enjoyed tennis and golf and sailing, too, when he had the time, although Helen had never been with him.

His eyes flickered over her wryly, and then he said: 'What's the panic? Who were you calling just then?'

Helen straightened from her lounging position by the telephone table and began to walk through to the lounge, running a smoothing hand over the loose curtain of her hair. 'There's no panic,' she replied in a taut little voice. 'And I was speaking to the office, actually. I wanted to know whether your—plans had changed.'

'My *plans*?' Jake crossed immediately to the cocktail cabinet and without hesitation poured himself a can of beer from the refrigerated compartment at the bottom. Swallowing half the contents of his glass, he turned back to her and raised his dark eyebrows. 'Why should I have changed my plans?'

Helen sighed, twisting her hands together. 'I thought perhaps—after this morning—I mean—'

Jake gave her a satirical stare and then flung himself into an armchair. 'You mean our little misunderstanding?' he queried mockingly. 'Now why should that change anything?'

'Oh, *Jake*!'

Helen felt she could slap that mocking expression from his face. He was deliberately amusing himself at her expense and she didn't like it.

Jake finished his beer and dropped the glass on to a glass-topped table. Then he drew out a case of cheroots and placed one between his lips. When it was lit, he regarded her through the smoke haze, watching the play of emotions on her expressive face.

'Don't take everything so seriously, Helen,' he advised her calmly.

'I thought that was what I was intended to do!' she exclaimed, stung by the mockery in his tones.

Jake's eyes narrowed. 'Perhaps you were at that,' he agreed lazily. 'In any event, I think we have satisfactorily disposed of the matter.'

'You've disposed of it!' cried Helen angrily.

'That's what I said,' replied Jake annoyingly.

'But I haven't!' Helen felt impotent. 'Look, Jake, I don't want to start another argument with you, but I refuse to be treated like an imbecile child! I'm a woman! I'm married to you, yes, I eat your food, and I spend your money! But even a housekeeper has some rights!'

Jake lay back in his chair with indolent grace, resting his dark head against the soft upholstery, and she felt an unexpected thrust of compassion for him. To see him there, his eyes half closed with weariness, so vulnerable somehow, disturbed her in a way she had hitherto never been disturbed. It was difficult to remember he was not what he seemed, that she was allowing him sympathy which he never asked nor gave. He was not vulnerable; she was a fool if she ever thought he was.

'All right,' he said now, moving his head slowly from side to side against the golden velvet of the chair back. 'We won't argue about it any more.'

Helen pressed her palms together. That wasn't entirely the answer she had wanted to hear. He had successfully avoided the issue and suddenly she had no heart to arouse him again. On the contrary, a feeling of contrition was unwillingly sweeping over her at the knowledge that it was her fault that he had had no sleep for over twenty-four hours.

The thick lashes drooped over his eyes suddenly, and she realised he had fallen asleep. She stared at him almost incredulously, and was about to turn away when something made her stop and turn and look again.

She had never seen Jake asleep before and it was remarkable to see the change in his face. It looked more youthful, somehow, gentler, the harsh lines softened by relaxation.

She looked at him for several long minutes, unable to explain her reasons for so doing. She had the urge to loosen his collar and tie, but she was afraid she might wake him if she tried to do so, and make him aware of what she was doing. She had never touched him, and he had never touched her except on those rare occasions when he fastened a necklace about her throat or pinned a corsage to her gown. She had never done anything that necessitated her touching him, but she realised now that she wanted to do so.

She quivered. Maybe it had never occurred to her before or so strongly how firm and brown was his skin, or how thick and vital was his hair. She wondered what it would be like to run her fingers through his hair or smooth his brown flesh. She had never had such thoughts before about any man, and there was something unsettling about them. Here was a man who ruthlessly went after anything he wanted, spurning the ordinary decencies of living, and yet he was capable of arousing the most disturbing emotions inside her at a time when she should be hating him for his arrogance.

With a muffled exclamation, she went out of the room. Sympathy was one thing, but allowing such ridiculous thoughts to take root in her mind was positively stupid. She crossed the hall to the stairs. How amused Jake would have been if he had known what she was thinking! No matter how angry he might get about her involvement with Keith Mannering, she knew he considered her emotionally frigid. He did not believe she had it in her to feel anything deeply, except perhaps normal grief at her father's death. He had been around. He had known others of the group she had been friendly with all those years ago. He must have been told she would never tolerate any heavy petting or any other kind of intimate contact. Probably that was part of the reason he had chosen her for his wife; everything of Jake Howard's must be whole, in perfect condition.

She stared at herself agonisingly in her dressing table mirror. Was that really how he saw her? Was her Scandinavian fair beauty merely a suitable foil for his darkness, and did he consider her as cool as the icebergs from which such excessive fairness came? Was she indeed that kind of woman?

Her palms moistened, and she turned away from the mirror in disgust. What did it matter what kind of woman she was? She was Jake Howard's wife, and he was not the kind of man to cede any possession of his.

About half an hour later, while Helen was lying on her bed, there was a tap at her bedroom door, and going to answer it, Helen found Mrs Latimer outside holding a tray. Stepping back, she allowed her to enter, and the housekeeper put down the tray on a low table and said:

'I've brought your lunch, madam. Mr Howard is sleeping in the lounge and I didn't think you'd want me to disturb him. Of course, if you want me to serve the meal—'

'Of course not, Mrs Latimer. That's all right.' Helen gave a slight smile. 'Actually, I was going to ask you not to disturb my husband. He's very tired.'

'Yes, madam. Is there anything else you need?'

Helen glanced at the tray trying to show interest in the food. 'No, that's lovely, thank you,' she replied dismissingly, and Mrs Latimer nodded politely and left, closing the door behind her.

After she had gone, Helen sighed and glanced at her watch. It was after one and she would have to start thinking about packing soon. When Jake awoke, he would expect her to be prepared, and she knew he would leave his packing to Mrs Latimer, who mothered him to an annoying extent.

Crossing to the long fitted wardrobe, Helen swept back the sliding doors and surveyed the array of clothes that confronted her. What kind of country weekend was it likely to be? she wondered People could call all kinds of dwelling places country cottages, and occasionally when she had spent a weekend with Jennifer and Giles, while Jake was out of the country, she had found their place in Wiltshire just as luxurious and sophisticated as their town apartment.

So what was she to gather from the small amount of information Jake had given her? Would the Ndanas be likely to have somewhere small but opulent, or would they prefer a less imposing break away from the city?

She sighed again. Her best plan would be to

take clothes to cover every eventuality. She had no intention of asking Jake and possibly creating another subject for argument.

Mrs Latimer came back for the tray to find it virtually untouched, and she frowned when she saw Helen was in the process of folding an evening gown into a suitcase.

'I could have done all that, madam!' she exclaimed. 'If you'd just put out what you wanted to take, I'd have been pleased to do it.'

Helen looked up from her task and smiled. 'Well, thank you, Mrs Latimer, but as you can see I've nearly finished. Is Mr Howard's case packed?'

'Yes, madam. I did that this morning after he told me you'd be away for the weekend.'

'I see.' Helen smoothed her hands together. 'Is Mr Howard awake yet?'

'I don't know, madam. I haven't been into the lounge. I expect he'll be coming to bathe and change shortly. Do you want me to wake him?'

Helen shook her head. 'No, that won't be necessary, Mrs Latimer. I'll wake my husband myself if he's still asleep, which I doubt somehow.' She frowned doubtfully. 'I just hope I've packed everything I'm likely to need.'

Mrs Latimer smiled. 'It's only for a couple of days, after all, madam, And I doubt if they stand on much ceremony at Llandranog!'

'Llandranog!' exclaimed Helen, in surprise. 'Is that in Wales?'

'Yes, madam.'

'You mean—this cottage we're going to is at Llandranog?'

'Yes, madam. Didn't Mr Howard tell you?'

Helen coloured. 'No—no, actually, I didn't get around to asking him. There were—er— other considerations.' She shook her head bewilderedly. 'Llandranog. I didn't realise we were going so far!'

Mrs Latimer shrugged. 'Not so far really. I expect you'll use the motorway. It will only be when you actually get into Wales that you may find the roads rather twisty. Tom and I went there once for our holidays. It's a lovely piece of country!'

Helen wrinkled her nose. 'In summer maybe, Mrs Latimer. But this is October. Look at the weather!' A steady drizzle had begun to fall at lunchtime and now everywhere looked wet and miserable.

Mrs Latimer chuckled. 'Well, I shouldn't worry, if I were you, Mrs Howard. With Mr Howard at the wheel, you'll have no difficulties.'

Helen was about to say that it wasn't only the journey she was troubled about and then decided against it. It would not do to treat Mrs Latimer as a confidante. The housekeeper's first allegiance was to her employer, after all, and while she might like and respect Helen, Jake would always hold precedence.

Helen showered and changed before going downstairs. She dressed in slim-fitting mauve corded pants and a black round-necked sweater, above which the creamy flesh of her throat rose alluringly. She secured the heavy swathe of hair with a black velvet band, leaving it loose about her shoulders. She carried the coat she was to wear over one arm. It was one of her favourite garments: cream suede, its collar, cuffs and short hemline edged with gold-coloured fur. A glance at her watch told her it was a little after three as she crossed to the lounge and she found Mrs Latimer in the process of placing a tray of tea on the low table before the couch.

She straightened when she saw Helen, and while Helen was registering that her husband was no longer lounging in the armchair, she said: 'Mr Howard thought you might like some tea before leaving.'

Helen threw her coat over the arm of a chair. 'That was thoughtful of him,' she remarked, the sarcasm only lightly veiled, and Mrs Latimer looked at her sharply, only to find Helen's expression unrevealing.

Still, the tea was welcome, Helen had to concede, and she was drinking her second cup when Jake appeared, looking big and disturbing in close-fitting suede trousers that hugged the

muscular length of his legs, and a knitted woollen
shirt that had a laced fastening at the neck. As
his clothes were dark they accentuated the darkness of his colouring, and Helen paused to wonder
whether there was any Spanish blood in his veins.
Then she half smiled. His mother would be most
offended if she could know what Helen was thinking. She was intensely proud of her Yorkshire
heritage.

Jake noticed the amusement on Helen's face,
and he frowned suddenly. 'Exactly what is so
funny?' he inquired ominously.

Helen sobered. 'Nothing much.' She replaced
her cup in its saucer. 'Are you ready to go now
or do you want some tea?'

Jake hesitated, and then slid his arms into the
sleeves of the sheepskin jacket he was carrying,
draped over one shoulder. 'I'm ready,' he replied
shortly. 'Where is your suitcase?'

'My *suitcases* are upstairs,' retorted Helen,
standing up.

'Suitcases!' Jake shook his head impatiently.
'For heaven's sake, what are you taking?'

Helen ran the palms of her hands down the
sides of her trousers. 'Well, as you didn't tell me
anything about the Ndanas, not even that their
cottage was in Wales, or what kind of reception
we were likely to receive, I had to cater for every
possibility!'

'I see. But I gather Mrs Latimer has told you.'

At her inclination of her head, he chewed his lip thoughtfully. 'Okay, point taken. I'll bring them down. I don't suppose the boot will be filled to overflowing with what I'm taking.'

'Thank you.' The words stuck in Helen's throat, but Jake had already gone, loping up the staircase and out of hearing. By the time he returned, Helen had put on her coat and was standing, hands in pockets in the hall, her head tilted towards the stairs.

As Jake came down with the cases, Mrs Latimer came out of the kitchen and clicked her tongue annoyedly. 'Now Tom could have brought them down, Mr Howard,' she exclaimed. 'He's just sitting in the kitchen drinking tea!'

Jake grinned at her, the kind of warm indulgence he reserved for people in his service evident in his expression. 'That's all right, Mrs Latimer,' he replied calmly. 'I'm not in my dotage yet.' He looked abruptly at Helen. 'Have you anything else to do?'

Helen frowned. 'I don't think so—oh! Oh, yes! The dinner engagement on Sunday! I shall have to cancel it.' In all the confusion of the day she had forgotten all about Jennifer.

Jake's expression became bleak. 'You have a dinner engagement for Sunday?' he inquired coldly.

Helen wanted to put out her tongue at him at

the derision in his voice. 'Yes,' she said deliberately. 'Yes, I have!'

Jake strode towards the door. 'Well, cancel it!'
he commanded harshly, and swinging open the
door went out with the cases, slamming the door
to behind him.

Mrs Latimer looked almost reproachfully at
Helen, but Helen was in no mood to placate her
by an explanation, so she said: 'I'll just make a
phone call, Mrs Latimer. You can go. I suppose
you know we expect to be back on Sunday
evening.'

'Yes, madam.' Mrs Latimer's tones were
clipped. 'Excuse me, madam.'

'Of course.'

Helen watched her go with impatience, and
then lifted the telephone receiver. As luck would
have it, Jennifer was in and she expressed instant
regret at Helen's news.

'But, darling, this is a new departure, for him,
isn't it?' she exclaimed, after Helen had explained
where they were going. 'I've never known him
take you along on one of these trips.'

Helen sighed. 'No, nor have I. But obviously
this is something special and he wants to give the
appearance of being a happily married man, I
suppose.'

'And do you think you're going to enjoy it?'
Jennifer sounded disparaging. 'I mean, darling, a

cottage in Wales, miles from civilisation! God, what a prospect!'

Helen made some polite rejoinder, and Jennifer went on: 'I mean, it wouldn't be so bad if you and Jake—well—if you were a normal married couple. It could be quite a giggle, couldn't it? But knowing that husband of yours, I should suspect the worst! You'll probably be left to the care of this Ambassador's wife while the Ambassador and Jake talk shop all the time. Either that or they'll disappear to some night spot, if there are such things there, and you'll be left to twiddle your thumbs.' She yawned, and then apologised. 'Honestly, darling, I don't know why you agreed to go in the first place! Let him do his own soliciting!'

Helen heard Jake coming back inside. 'Look, I've got to go,' she said quickly. 'I'll give you a ring when we get back.'

Jennifer sighed irritably. 'Oh, very well, Helen. But don't blame me if you come back with pneumonia, or chilblains, or both!'

'I won't.' Helen rang off hastily and Jake gave her a raking stare.

'Well?' he said. 'Are you ready now?'

'Of course.' Helen held up her head defiantly. She would not allow him to intimidate her in this way. She refused to stammer out explanations like a frightened child, just because he expected them.

They were driving to the cottage in Jake's

Ferrari. He used the limousine around town, but when he was driving himself any distance he preferred the sleek sports car. Helen had only been in the Ferrari about half a dozen times, and then only for short distances. As Jennifer had pointed out so disparagingly, this weekend was a new departure for Jake, and Helen could only assume, as she had said, that her husband needed the steadiness of his marriage as a potent demonstration of his reliability to Ndana. African politicians were invariably family men and considered the free and easy attitude of the western world towards sex a symbol of a decadent society.

For the first hour of their journey Jake was too intent upon his driving to pay much attention to Helen. It was raining quite heavily now and in the rush-hour traffic of a Friday evening it was impossible to relax one's concentration. But once they were out of the thick of it and on to the motorway, Jake visibly eased his long body into a more comfortable position and lit a cheroot. Then he glanced towards his wife, and said:

'What did Mannering say?'

Helen chose to be obtuse, her fingers clasped together in her lap, her green eyes never leaving the road. 'Mannering?' she asked, with assumed surprise.

Jake's long fingers tightened momentarily on the wheel, and then he said, almost pleasantly: 'Don't try to be clever with me, Helen. You ought to know by now that it just doesn't work. I asked you what Mannering said when you had to tell him you couldn't dine with him on Sunday evening.'

'Oh, *that*!' Helen shrugged her shoulders annoyingly.

'Yes, that!' Jake's voice was grim now.

'He didn't say anything.'

'Helen, I warn you—'

Helen looked his way then her eyes flashing angrily. 'For goodness' sake, Jake,' she exclaimed, 'stop acting the heavy father! For your information, I did not have a dinner date with Keith Mannering for Sunday evening!'

'Do you expect me to believe that?'

'Please yourself!' Helen returned her attention to the road, fuming because she had allowed him to get her so angry that she had automatically defended herself.

'Then who were you telephoning?'

'Oh, for heaven's sake!' Helen looked mutinously at him. 'Why should I tell you who I was phoning? What does it matter? I don't ask you about your activities, so why should you know everything about mine?'

Suddenly, a heavy lorry pulled out into the fast-moving lane and Jake had to brake hard as the awkward vehicle blocked his path. The incident momentarily eased the tension between them. Helen had to concede that Jake was a very competent driver, handling the powerful car with an expertise which she could have enjoyed in other circumstances. Indeed this whole weekend could have been a delightful experience—she had never been to Wales before—and casting a surreptitious glance at Jake she wondered how many girls would have given almost anything to be in her position, looking at things from a wholly superficial angle, of course. She found herself assessing her husband in a purely physical way and had to accept that he was a disturbingly masculine animal.

With determination she stared out of the window at the unremitting wall of rain that enveloped them. Since Jake's return from the States three weeks ago and their subsequent confrontations she was becoming far too conscious of him, and she tried to drum up the feeling of revulsion she had always cocooned herself in whenever she considered his ruthless nature. He was not like the men she was accustomed to, she told herself fiercely. He was coarse, and crude, satisfying his male appetites in whatever manner suited him best, ignoring the codes of honour and decency she had been brought up to respect. And certainly he had no respect for her sex. Women might serve a useful purpose for him, but as individuals he had little time for them. Any woman who was foolish enough to get involved with Jake Howard need expect nothing from him. Only she, as his wife, had received a small measure of indifferent regard; she was inviolate, protected, supported, but, it appeared, only so long as she lived a completely obedient and blameless existence. And if ever she was foolish enough to imagine that her position gave her any advantages over any other woman she had no doubt Jake would do everything in his power to disabuse her of that belief.

The lorry eventually pulled into the slow lane and Jake stood on the accelerator, passing everything in sight with an ease which was in itself exhilarating. They travelled on in silence for some time, both occupied with their own thoughts, but Helen was shaken out of her apathy by Jake pulling off the motorway and followed an invitingly signposted side road to a large hotel, whose lights gleamed warmly through the misted windows.

'I thought we'd have dinner,' remarked Jake shortly, unfastening his seat belt. 'It's early, I know, only about half past six, but I thought it would save us stopping later on roads we don't know.'

Helen nodded, and unfastening her own seat belt stepped out of the car in relief. It was good to stretch her legs, and not even the steady downpour spoiled the moment for her. She tucked up her collar, framing her face with the soft fur, and after Jake had locked the car they walked the few yards to the lighted entrance to the building.

Inside it was warmly comfortable, and they shed their coats in the lobby and walked into the restaurant together. Although it was early, several diners were already enjoying their meal, and they glanced rather curiously at Helen and Jake as they were shown to their table. Certainly Jake would attract attention anywhere, thought Helen wryly, scarcely aware of the charming picture she presented in the close-fitting slacks and softly clinging sweater.

Jake was morose throughout the meal, speaking seldom and only when Helen made some comment about the meal. She felt she had to say something if only to prove to the interested spectators around them that they were on speaking terms.

Finally, when they were having liqueurs with their coffee, and Jake was smoking a deliciously smelling Havana cigar, she said heatedly: 'If you must know, I was speaking to Jennifer on the telephone before we left. It was she who had invited us *both* for dinner on Sunday evening!'

Jake did not reply, and Helen grew impatient. 'Did you hear what I said?' she exclaimed in a low, angry tone.

Jake's dark lashes flickered upwards. 'Yes, I heard, Helen.'

'Well, haven't you anything to say?'

'What do you want me to say?'

Helen compressed her lips bitterly, aware that

she was near to tears suddenly. How ridiculous, she thought impatiently. Just because he had chosen to sulk over their argument she had given in yet again and given him another opportunity to humiliate her.

Without answering him, she got to her feet and pushing back her chair she walked abruptly out of the room. She grabbed her coat from its hook by the outer door and tugging it carelessly over her shoulders she went outside, hesitating as the cold draught of wind and rain showered her relentlessly. But she could hardly stand in the hotel doorway, and thrusting her arms into the sleeves of her coat she stepped out into the storm, gasping as the chill wind caught her breath.

She walked blindly towards the Ferrari, but of course it was locked and she had no key. She fastened her coat, pushing her hands deep into the pockets, trying to prevent her lips from trembling by biting them. She had never felt more wretched in all her young life.

The sound of the hotel door banging behind her caused her to glance round apprehensively and she saw Jake striding towards her, purposefully. He raked her with a merciless glance, noticing her damp hair clinging in tendrils to her wet face, dejected hunching of her slim shoulders, the unhappy droop of her mouth, and without a word he unlocked the car door and taking her arm thrust her abruptly inside. Then he slammed

the door and walked swiftly round the bonnet to
climb in beside her, sliding a hand through the
thickness of his own hair which was inclined to
curl when it was wet.

Then he turned towards her in his seat, and
she waited with bated breath for the angry tirade
which was to follow. But just when her nerves
were stretched to screaming pitch, he said in a
low half reluctant tone: 'All right, all right, Helen.
I'm sorry!'

Helen turned her head to look at him, her eyes
wide and incredulous. 'You're—you're sorry?'
she echoed faintly.

'Yes! Yes, goddammit, what more do you want
me to say? Okay, I'm a swine! I didn't believe
you. Now I do.'

'Oh, *Jake*!'

To her horror, Helen felt the hot tears squeez-
ing through her lids at his words, running
treacherously down her face. He must have sus-
pected something was wrong when she scrubbed
the palms of her hands painfully across her cheeks
in an effort to hide her distress and he switched
on the interior light, staring at her with a curious
look in his eyes.

'For God's sake, Helen,' he muttered forcefully, 'I've said I'm sorry. Don't cry, for heaven's
sake! I'm not worth it, believe me!'

Helen moved her head slowly from side to side.
'Just leave me alone. I'll be all right,' she insisted

chokingly, her palms pressed to her mouth.

'Ah, Helen—*woman*—be still!' he groaned, almost under his breath, and he slid an arm about her shoulders, pulling her close to him so that she buried her face against his chest. It was the first time she had been this close to him, and for several minutes she was content just to lie there, feeling the all-enveloping security of his nearness.

But gradually, as her tears subsided, Helen became aware of other sensations that were just as disastrous to her peace of mind. The warmth of Jake's skin penetrated the fine woollen material of his sweater, and she was intensely conscious of the hard strength of his body and the clean, male smell of him. And while she knew she ought to move away from him and dry her eyes, she didn't want to do so.

But the initiative was taken out of her hands by Jake himself taking her by the shoulders and propelling her gently but firmly back into her own seat. Then he flicked out the interior light, put a cheroot between his lips and lit it with swift, sure movements, and finally turned on the ignition.

The powerful engine roared to life and glancing briefly over his shoulder to make sure it was clear, Jake swung the car round in a semi-circle and made for the exit. He did not speak, and soon the lights of the motorway engulfed them.

But Helen lay in her seat, tremblingly aware

that for the first time in her life she would not have found the touch of a man's hands undesirable. . .

CHAPTER FIVE

THE road uncoiled before them, wet and gleaming, reptilian in its writhing persistence. They had left the comparative simplicity of the motorway far behind now, and were penetrating further and further into wild, hilly country where not even an occasional village interrupted their solitary passage. Perhaps it might not have seemed so bad in daylight, thought Helen doubtfully, but in the pouring rain and almost complete darkness it was all slightly unnerving.

Since leaving the hotel car park, Jake had spoken little and then usually to ask Helen to check the map to ensure they were not on the wrong road. She had wondered whether he was regretting his momentary softening earlier; certainly there was no sign of compassion now in the grim lines of his features. But he was having to use all his undoubted skill to keep the powerful car from skidding on the hair-raising bends, and from time to time he cursed softly under his breath as he had to use his gears to reduce his speed.

Helen just wished they were at their destination. She longed to get out of the close proximity of the car, away from Jake's disturbing presence, away from the probing intimacy of her thoughts that seduced her mind so that she found herself noticing every little thing about her husband; the thick length of his lashes, the almost cruel lines of his profile, the way his hair grew low on his neck, the hairs on his wrists protruding from the sleeves of his sweater where his watch gleamed dully. These things had never disturbed her before and she loathed herself when she considered that she could allow herself to feel this way when she knew that only two nights ago. . .

She shivered involuntarily, and he glanced her way. 'Cold?' he inquired, his tones abrupt.

Helen shook her head. 'Someone walked over my grave,' she denied, with assumed lightness. 'How much longer do you think we'll be before we get there?'

Jake glanced at his watch. 'I thought we'd have been there by now,' he remarked frowningly. 'Are you sure this is the right road?'

Helen leant forward and extracted the map from its compartment. Switching on the interior light, she quickly scanned the area they were negotiating.

'This is the Llandranog road,' she asserted firmly. 'It has to be.'

'Does it?' Jake sounded less convinced. 'In God's name, why don't they signpost their roads more thoroughly? It must be ten miles since I saw any sign of where we might be.'

'We could have missed the signposts in the dark,' suggested Helen cautiously. 'After all, it is raining—'

'Thank you, I had noticed.' Jake was barely civil.

Helen switched out the interior light again, and subsided into silence again. Presently, however, she sat up again and pointed excitedly. 'I can see lights. Look—there! Can you see them?'

Jake gave her a quelling stare. 'Yes, I can see them. But that doesn't look like a village to me. It looks more like a solitary dwelling.'

Helen hunched her shoulders. 'Well, it ought to be Llandranog!' she said, rather resentfully. 'According to the map—'

'All right, all right.' Jake swung the car on to the right-hand side of the road to avoid the sharpness of the bend they were cornering, and now ahead of them they could both see the lights quite clearly. But as Jake had said, the lights were few and scarcely sufficient to signify a whole village.

'Maybe everyone's gone to bed,' Helen murmured tentatively.

'At nine-thirty?' Jake gave her a derogatory glance. 'I rather doubt it, somehow, don't you?'

'Then perhaps you ought to do your own navigating!' snapped Helen, stung by his sarcasm.

'Perhaps I have,' Jake returned, and then he stepped gently on his brakes and brought the car to a halt. 'Do you see what I see?'

Helen looked through the streaming windows. Now that they were nearer she could see that the lights did indeed signify a house, but the house was not even on the road but some distance away up a muddy track.

'There's a name on that gatepost,' she pointed out hopefully.

Jake heaved a sigh, looked at her for a long moment, and then inclined his head. 'Okay, okay—I'll go see what it says.'

Helen nodded and Jake thrust open his door and stepped out. Immediately his suede boot sank ankle deep into mud and Helen heard his angry ejaculation before he slammed the door behind him and squelched away towards the gate.

Helen felt the beginnings of a giggle rising in her throat and hastily quelled it. But to imagine Jake stepping out carelessly into several inches of mud was suddenly irresistibly funny. Maybe it was reaction after the journey, but whatever it was she must not allow Jake to see that she was amused at his discomfort. She only hoped he was not going to be too angry when he got back.

However her hopes were doomed to disappointment: Jake was angry, furiously angry, and he climbed into the car abruptly without even bothering to clean the mud off his boots.

'Do you have any idea what it says on that gatepost?' he demanded, the interior light illuminating the hardness of his features. 'It says—wait for it! Llangranog Farm! Do you understand me? Llan*granog*!'

Helen's brows drew together in a puzzled frown. 'You mean that that is the cottage?' she questioned innocently.

Jake raised his eyes heavenward in a expressive gesture of disgust. 'No,' he snapped, 'I do not mean that that is the cottage. I mean that that building is Llangranog Farm! Not Llandranog!'

Helen's lips parted and her eyes widened in understanding. 'You mean—you mean—this— is the road to Llangranog, and not Llandranog?'

Jake tapped his fingers impatiently against the steering wheel. 'Do I? Well, you ought to know— you've been navigating!'

Helen fumbled for the map, spreading it out on her knees with trembling fingers. She traced the line of their route since leaving the motorway, finding, without much difficulty, the twisting mountainous road they had followed. But her finger faltered as she realised she had indeed been following the signs for Llangranog by mistake. She had not thought there could be two names so much alike and because the road to Llangranog was the major road she had not observed the turn-off for Llandranog some distance back.

Jake had been following her probing finger with his eyes and when she looked up tremulously she found him regarding her with something like exasperation in his face.

'How far out of our way have we come?' he asked tolerantly, and Helen turned her attention hastily to the map.

'A—about fifteen miles,' she stammered unhappily.

Jake sighed and lay back in his seat, reaching for his cigars. 'Okay,' he said, without rancour, 'we'll go back.'

'I'm—I'm sorry.' Helen bit her lip. 'I didn't think there'd be two names so much alike.'

Jake's lips twisted in an imitation of a smile. 'Nor did I,' he conceded dryly. 'I can't altogether blame you. I looked at the road signs, too.'

Helen gave a slight smile. 'Thank you.'

He shook his head deprecatingly and flicking the starter set off the powerful engine again. But when he put the car into gear and released the clutch, the rear wheels spun uselessly.

Pressing his lips together determinedly, Jake thrust the gear lever into reverse, but again only the soft swishing noise of wheels spinning uselessly in mud came to them over the roar of the engine.

'Oh, God!' Jake's fingers clenched on the wheel. 'Now how the hell are we going to get out of this?'

Helen chewed helplessly at her lips. She couldn't help feeling it was all her fault and she wished there was something she could do. Jake thrust open his door and climbed out again, but this time Helen felt no amusement as he squelched into the mud. He slammed the door and went round to the rear of the vehicle and she felt him kick the tyres with an impatient boot. Then he came back again and said:

'Get into the driving seat, Helen, and take off the brake. Put it into gear and rev hard on the accelerator when I tell you to, right?'

'All right.' Helen climbed obediently into the driving seat, but her legs wouldn't reach the pedals. 'Wait!' she called anxiously, and Jake came back to her, his hair wet and curling now.

'What's the matter?' he asked shortly.

Helen pointed to her legs. 'The seat's too far back for me. Can you lever it forward?'

Jake sighed, but he bent and with a swift movement brought the seat nearer to the pedals. 'Is that okay?'

Helen tried it. 'Well, I can manage,' she agreed.

'Good. Let's get on, shall we? Now remember, when I say go—*go*!'

'Yes, Jake!' Helen was meek.

'Good!'

Jake walked back to the rear of the car and glancing through the rain-misted rear screen she saw him bracing himself against the back of the vehicle.

'All right!' he called, and Helen released the

clutch, pressing hard on the accelerator as she did so.

But the wheels still spun and there was an exclamation of disgust from Jake before he called: 'All right, all right! Pack it in!'

Helen leaned out of the window and saw Jake coming towards her. He was splattered from head to foot with mud and the stupid giggle she had suppressed earlier burst out of her without volition. Immediately, she was horrified and pressed a hand to her mouth, but not before he had seen her amusement.

He halted beside the window regarding her intently. 'You find it amusing, do you?' he queried ominously.

Helen shook her head, scarcely trusting herself to speak. 'You—you're covered in mud!' she said awkwardly. 'I'm sorry, Jake, but you did look funny.'

'Did I?' Jake wiped wet hands over his face, grunting as his hands became smeared with mud. 'Okay, beautiful, you try it!'

Helen stared at him incredulously. 'Me?' she gasped. 'You're not serious!'

'Why not? You got us into this mess. You get us out.'

Helen climbed back into her own seat. 'I'm not going to get covered in mud just to give you a laugh!'

Jake hesitated, and then glanced up the track

to where Llangranog Farm was illuminated. 'I wonder if the owner of the farm has anything we could use to get out of here. We're practically in the ditch now after that last little episode.'

Helen was so relieved that he was not going to force her to push the car that she blabbered enthusiastically, 'Oh, yes, perhaps. Maybe he'll have a tractor and a rope or something. He could pull us out. Oh, that's a good idea.'

Jake opened the car door. 'Good. I thought you'd think so. Go and ask him!'

Helen's mouth dropped open. 'Me?' she exclaimed again. 'Go up to the farm?'

'Yes.' Jake lit another cheroot. 'I'll wait here in case anyone happens along.'

Helen pursed her lips. 'I can't go to the farm,' she insisted. 'It's up that track! Heavens, there might be somebody up there just waiting for someone like me!'

'In this downpour? I doubt it.' Jake was complacent.

'Oh, you're not serious!' Helen stared at him hopefully. 'You're just saying this to frighten me! I think you're mean!'

'I am serious, Helen.' Jake unloosened his coat deliberately. 'And what's more, you're going to do it!'

'I refuse!' Helen held up her head haughtily.

'Do you? Do you really?'

Without warning, Jake leant past her and thrust

open her door and bundled her out, pushing her
coat into her hands and slamming the door again
and locking it from the inside so that she could
not get back in. Helen was horrified, but common
sense made her put on her coat before she began
banging frantically on the window.

'Jake, stop being so rotten! Let me in! I'm
getting soaked!'

'Run up to the farm, then,' he shouted back at
her. 'Go on! The exercise will do you good!'

Helen hesitated uncertainly. She knew Jake
well enough to know that he meant what he said,
but she could scarcely accept it. How could she
go up to a strange house and ask the owner to
turn out to get them out of a ditch? It could be
some man living alone, anybody!

She shivered and stared angrily at Jake, smoking unconcernedly inside the low-slung sports
car. She thought she hated him. Hunching her
shoulders, she put up her collar and stared through
the gloom towards the lane to the farm. She was
already standing in mud. What would the lane be
like? Thoughts of animals going up and down the
lane filled her mind, and she thought disgustedly
of the manure they made.

But it was simply no good standing there waiting for Jake to change his mind. She should know
by now that he didn't play the game by any rules
but his own, and just because she was a woman
she need expect no favours from him.

With ill-grace she turned and walked towards the lane, tears of exasperation and humiliation and simple honest fear running down her cheeks. The house seemed a long way up the lane, but she might as well accept that she had to go or stand here getting soaked for possibly hours.

She began to trudge up the lane, avoiding any dark patches on the ground which might have been anything. The wind tore through her hair, and the rain soaked it to her head, and she felt utterly miserable. She wished for the first time she had taken Jennifer's advice and told Jake to visit the Ndanas on his own. Why should she be subjected to this kind of treatment just to please him? It wouldn't have been so bad if he had been gentlemanly about everything, but there he was, sitting comfortably in the car, while she was struggling up this filthy lane in a positive rainstorm.

As she neared the farmyard, she heard the sound of animals in a nearby barn, and the unmistakable barking of a dog heralding her arrival. But more disturbingly, behind her, she heard the sound of heavy breathing and the squelching sound of footsteps in the mud.

Panic swept through her, and she began to run wildly towards the curtained windows behind which a light burned brightly. But just as she reached the porch, a hand caught her arm and she gasped as Jake dragged her back and went forward himself to knock at the door.

'You—you pig!' she cried, in an undertone. 'You rotten pig! Have you been following me?'

Jake raised dark eyebrows, his face dark and saturnine in the lights from the farm. 'Of course. You didn't suppose I would let you come up here alone, did you?'

'But—but—' Helen moved her shoulders helplessly. 'Why did you make me come at all? Why couldn't you have left me in the car?'

Jake shrugged. 'Would you have wanted to be left there? Alone? In the dark? On that lonely road?'

'Well—'

'I decided to teach you a lesson, that was all.' Jake half smiled. 'I think I've succeeded, don't you?'

'Oh—oh, I *hate you*!' Helen put a wealth of feeling into her voice, and just then the door opened, and several dogs of various breeds surged out to jump excitedly round their legs.

The man who had opened the door bade the dogs get back inside in a commanding tone, and then looked curiously at his bedraggled visitors.

'Yes?' he said frowningly.

Jake stepped under cover of the porch. 'I'm sorry to trouble you at this time of night, but I'm afraid my car is stuck in a ditch at the end of your road. I wondered if I might prevail upon you to give us a tow.' He went on quickly: 'I—

I know it's late and a filthy evening, but—well—as you can see, my wife and I are soaked to the skin.'

The man looked thoughtfully at Helen's hopeful face and the way she was shivering quite uncontrollably, and then he stepped back abruptly and said: 'You'd better come in. Your lady looks as though a cup of tea wouldn't come amiss.'

'Oh, thank you!' Helen stepped forward eagerly, a smile lifting the corners of her mouth, her expression warm with gratitude, and the elderly farmer made a modest movement of his shoulders.

'It is nothing,' he said, closing the door behind them, and then leading the way across a wood-tiled hall into a large, comfortable living room where a huge fire burned brightly, filling the room with warmth and the sweet smell of logs.

His wife was a small, plump woman, the epitome of everything a farmer's wife should be. After they had introduced themselves as Mr and Mrs Morgan, and Helen and Jake had given their names in return, Mrs Morgan disappeared to make some tea while her husband questioned Jake about what had happened.

'You're not the first to make that mistake,' he nodded smilingly, as Jake explained about the mix-up over the names. 'There has always been trouble over it. But there, I'm sure you're not interested in that.' He frowned. 'Your car's stuck

in the ditch, you say? Well, I could get out the
tractor and pull you out, but it's all going to take
time and perhaps these friends you are going to
spend the weekend with will be wondering where
you are. Perhaps it would be better if you telephoned them and explained what had happened,
and then stayed here tonight. In the morning it
might have stopped raining, and you'll easily find
the turn off for Llandranog. In the dark—well,
you could miss it again.'

Jake glanced at Helen. 'That's very kind of
you, Mr Morgan,' he began, 'but we couldn't put
you to the trouble—'

'Now, I'm sure Mrs Morgan would agree with
me, it's no trouble.' The old farmer grinned cheerfully. 'We don't get many visitors here, and our
own family are grown up now and married with
families of their own. There's plenty of room,
and I'm sure Mrs Howard doesn't fancy trailing
back down that track again tonight, do you,
my dear?'

Helen bit her lip, and then looked at Jake, not
really knowing what to answer. She could think
of nothing more desirable than staying here
beside this warm fire for the rest of the evening
and then making her way to a comfortable bed
without braving the weather again. But what
would Jake think? Would he want to press on?
After all, the Ndanas were not like ordinary
friends.

Jake was frowning now. He had shed his sheep skin coat and was sitting at the other side of the fire, the fire drying his hair, so that it fell rather attractively across his forehead. He, too, looked warm and relaxed, and she wondered what his thoughts were at that moment.

'I—I don't know what to say—' Helen was beginning, when Jake said:

'I really think we ought to press on, Mr Morgan. It's going to put you to a lot of trouble—'

Mrs Morgan returned at that moment with a tray on which was a pot of tea and four cups, and a delicious bowl of beef broth. She ladled some into dishes as her husband explained to her what he had been saying, and then she said:

'Now you know it's no trouble at all. Like Owen says, we'd be glad of a bit of company. You can't honestly expect to go any further tonight.'

Helen looked across at Jake. 'Are—our friends—on the telephone?' she queried awkwardly.

Jake's dark eyes bored into hers. 'Yes, they're on the phone,' he agreed shortly.

'Then—couldn't we do as Mr Morgan suggests and stay?' Helen managed a slight smile. 'After all, it would be easier to find the cottage in the morning.'

Jake's lips twisted. 'I'm sure it would,' he

confirmed dryly. 'However, I thought you wanted
to get there.'

Helen's brows drew together. 'Me? No, not
particularly. Why?'

Jake's eyes were glinting slightly. 'Very well,
if you don't want to go on,' he said.

Helen tried to control her impatience. Jake was
deliberately making it her decision. Why?

'I'm perfectly happy to stay here,' she told
him curtly.

'Good. Then I'll go and get the cases.' He
stood up.

'No, wait, boy!' Mr Morgan got to his feet.
'It's pretty wet out there. I'm sure for one night
you could manage without your cases. Dilys can
find something for your wife to wear, I'm sure,
and I've got pyjamas which should do for you.'

Jake hesitated. Then he seemed to come to a
decision, for he sat down again, and finished the
cup of tea Mrs Morgan had poured for him. 'All
right,' he said. 'I'm sure we both appreciate your
kindness, don't we, Helen?'

Helen nodded, but she would have liked to
have added that while she appreciated what the
Morgans were doing, she did not altogether
appreciate her husband's attitude. He seemed to
be enjoying some joke at her expense, his earlier
brusqueness having given way to a sardonic indifference which was difficult to understand.

Mrs Morgan took their coats away to dry in

the kitchen and Mr Morgan showed Jake where he could make his telephone call. Helen sat on by the fire, her hair almost dry and shining in the fire-light. She felt warm and contented and when Mrs Morgan returned she chatted quite amicably to her about her home in London and the appalling state of the weather. Mrs Morgan in her turn told Helen about the three sons and two daughters she had brought up and how she now had nineteen grandchildren. Helen was interested and when Jake returned she was engrossed in the family snap album with both the Morgans.

'That's all right,' Jake said in explanation, as he came back into the room. 'They'll expect us soon after breakfast in the morning.'

'Good, good!' Mr Morgan nodded and smiled, and accepted the cigar Jake offered him.

It could have been such a pleasant evening, but Helen was intensely conscious of Jake's manner and she wondered if this was his way of showing his disapproval. Later Mrs Morgan disappeared to prepare their rooms, and Helen was surprised to see it was almost eleven o'clock.

Looking at Mr Morgan, she exclaimed: 'We mustn't keep you up, Mr Morgan. I'm sure you have an early start in the morning.'

Mr Morgan shook his head. 'Not as early as I used to, Mrs Howard. My sons do most of the hard work about the place now. I'm just the gaffer.' He chuckled.

Helen smiled. 'I expect you love it here,' she volunteered.

'Oh, in summer it's marvellous!' he agreed. 'Have you ever been to the Welsh mountains before, Mrs Howard?'

'I've not even been to Wales before,' replied Helen. 'But if all the people are as friendly as you and Mrs Morgan then I shall certainly come again.'

The old man looked touched by her submission and Jake's expression grew more sardonic than ever.

Eventually Mrs Morgan returned. 'When you're ready, I'll show you to your bed,' she said smilingly. 'I've laid out some night-clothes for you, but you can please yourselves whether you use them!' She raised her eyebrows teasingly, and for the first time Helen felt a twinge of apprehension.

Of *course*! Why hadn't she thought of it before? To the Morgans they were a normal married couple! She stared accusingly at Jake, and he allowed his lids to narrow slightly at the look in her eyes. *You beast*! she wanted to storm at him. *You knew*! That was why Jake had looked so derisively at her earlier. He had guessed what the Morgans would think. *Oh, why hadn't she*?

As Mrs Morgan obviously expected them to retire now, Helen rose unhappily from her seat and Jake followed her out of the room after bidding goodnight to Mr Morgan, who nodded smilingly by the fire.

The stairs were winding and carpeted in a rough woven carpet that was hard to Helen's stockinged feet. Both she and Jake had shed their muddy shoes and left them to dry downstairs.

The room Mrs Morgan showed them into was large and high-ceilinged, and contained an enormous double bed of the type Helen had not seen outside of antique shops. Lying on the pillows was a capacious nightgown for Helen and a pair of flannelette pyjamas for Jake.

'I think you'll be comfortable here,' Mrs Morgan was saying anxiously. 'I've put hot water bottles in the bed, and there's a couple of extra blankets on the ottoman over there if you're cold.' Then she smiled at them both teasingly. 'But I'm sure you won't feel the cold, will you? Young things like you! When Owen and I were your age we used to keep one another warm.' She chuckled reminiscently. 'Now we rely on an electric blanket!'

Jake grinned. 'I'm sure this will do us very nicely, Mrs Morgan.'

Mrs Morgan nodded. 'Yes, I'm sure it will. Now the bathroom's across the hall—that door there!' She pointed across the landing. 'And there's plenty of hot water if either of you want a bath in the morning.'

'Thank you.' Helen was forced to say something, and with another encompassing smile Mrs Morgan went out, wishing them goodnight as she closed the door.

Only then did Helen turn to Jake, a look of sheer frustration on her face. '*You knew*!' she hissed fiercely. 'You knew the Morgans would only provide us with one room!'

Jake looked down mockingly into her shocked face. 'Of course I knew. And if you'd had any sense, you'd have realised it, too. But you were so wrapped up in an aura of warmth and well-being that you didn't stop to think, did you? Well, it serves you right! Not only do we have only one room, we have only one bed! And I, for one, do not intend sleeping on the floor!'

CHAPTER SIX

HELEN stared disbelievingly at him. 'What do you mean?'

Jake walked indolently across the carpeted floor. 'What do you think I mean? I thought I'd made it plain enough.'

Helen twisted her hands behind her back. 'You—intend—to use—the bed?' she ventured unhappily.

Jake turned. He had reached the side of the bed and he lifted the flannelette pyjamas from the pillow with a mocking hand, holding them up with assumed puzzlement. 'Now what do you suppose these are?' he inquired musingly.

Helen pressed her lips together. 'Oh, stop fooling about, Jake!' she snapped irritably. 'What are we going to do?'

Jake sat down on his side of the bed and began to unfasten his shirt under her horrified gaze. 'I don't know what you're about to do, Helen. But I am going to bed. You may recall, I didn't sleep at all last night, and I have no intention of suffering the same fate tonight.'

'But, Jake. . .' Helen spread a helpless hand,

walking about the room restlessly. 'We can't both sleep in this room!'

Jake shrugged, pulling off his shirt to reveal the brown muscular expanse of his chest, liberally covered with hair. Helen looked away abruptly. She had never seen him without a shirt. They had never had a holiday together and consequently she had not seen him in swimming gear. But it was obvious from the tan of his skin that he had not spent all his time in the United States in the boardroom. In consequence, she was terse when she exclaimed:

'For goodness' sake, Jake! Put the pyjama jacket on!'

Jake tossed the pyjamas carelessly to the foot of the bed. Then he lay back, stretching his arms back above his head with abandoned ease. 'You wear them,' he advised her lazily. 'I never use the things myself.'

Helen gave an exclamation of frustration. 'You—you can't mean to—to—'

Jake turned his head sideways so that his eyes flickered over her startled face with wry amusement. 'I can't mean to what? Sleep in the raw?' He smiled mockingly. 'No—I won't shock your puritan little soul to that extent.'

Helen moved to the massive dressing table, unwillingly laying her handbag down and removing the band of velvet from her hair so that it fell about her face in a soft curtain. Then she held back her hair with one hand and surveyed her reflection in the mirror without pleasure.

Jake sat up, and yawned. 'Do you want to use the bathroom?' he queried matter-of-factly, and she swung round on him.

'You're enjoying this, aren't you?' she accused him in a low angry voice. 'You don't care about my feelings at all!'

Jake's expression hardened slightly and he rose to his feet. 'Now, Helen,' he said flatly. 'You got us into this. It's up to you to make the best of it.'

'But we can't share the bed,' she protested.

'Why not?' His eyes probed hers and she flushed hotly. 'Contrary to your beliefs, I do find some things more important than my—animal needs! That was what you once called them, wasn't it?' He frowned. 'Right now, all I want to do is sleep!'

Helen moved reluctantly towards the bed, lifting the nightdress doubtfully. It too was made of flannelette, and she could see it would be several sizes too big for her. She shook it out and Jake's lips twitched.

'I should plump for the pyjamas!' he remarked dryly. 'At least they have a cord.'

Helen pressed her lips together tightly. 'And what are you going to wear?'

Jake shrugged. 'Don't worry about me. I'll manage.'

Helen heaved a sigh. 'I don't want to go to the

bathroom. You go—and I'll get into bed.'

Jake regarded her for a long moment and then he nodded. 'All right, Modesty Blaise! But please, don't take too long.'

Helen waited until the door was closed and then she hastily stripped off her trousers and sweater and tights. The pyjama trousers were much too big for her, but at least, as Jake had pointed out, they had a cord, and she secured it tightly about her waist before pulling on the huge jacket.

She didn't stop to see what she looked like, but drew back the covers and climbed swiftly into the big bed. Her toes encountered the hot water bottle at her feet and she sighed luxuriously. In other circumstances she would have felt wonderfully warm and comfortable.

Jake came back a few minutes later, walking into the bedroom unannounced, and she stared at him resentfully.

'Well, I could hardly knock before entering my wife's bedroom, could I?' he remarked logically, when he encountered her indignation.

Helen made no reply, turning abruptly on to her side away from him, and with a shrug he went to turn out the light. A few moments later she felt the bed give on his side as the weight of his body was added to the lightness of hers.

She moved as far away from him as possible, keeping to her own side of the bed, her body stiff and unyielding, half afraid that he might choose to ignore what he had told her earlier.

But after only a few minutes, she heard his breathing deepen, and she realised with a ridiculous sense of anti-climax that he was asleep. . .

It seemed to take Helen hours to get to sleep. Clinging to the edge of the mattress was not a particularly comfortable position in which to try and relax, and her indignation against Jake increased when he moved lazily in his sleep, turning on to his back and spreading himself into the space she had left between them, not even stirring when he touched her still form.

Helen kept her eyes tightly closed, willing him to move away, but he seemed completely unaware of her. Probably, she thought with revulsion, he was not unused to having a woman share his bed, but she had always slept alone, and hot tears of self-pity stung her eyes once again, only to be dashed away by an impatient finger.

Eventually, sheer exhaustion overtook her and she slept, not waking until the sound of Mrs Morgan coming into the room with a tray of morning tea disturbed her. Even then she was loath to move, and as her eyes flickered open she realised why she had felt so warm and comfortable. During the night she must have felt cold, and she had snuggled up to Jake and she now lay close in the small of his back, one arm curved round his waist.

With an exclamation of surprise, she withdrew her arm sharply, and struggled into a sitting position, managing to return Mrs Morgan's cheerful smile. Jake did not stir, and Mrs Morgan whispered:

'It's not raining any more, Mrs Howard. Now tell me, did you sleep all right?'

Helen coloured, drawing the huge pyjama jacket protectively about her. 'Thank you, very well,' she returned softly. 'And thank you for the tea.'

Mrs Morgan placed the tray on the table beside her. 'Now that's nothing at all. What will your husband have for his breakfast? Eggs and bacon? Some sausages, perhaps?'

Helen glanced at Jake, and as though aware of her gaze he stirred, stretching a little. 'That— that would be fine, Mrs Morgan,' she murmured, wishing the woman would go so that she could get out of the bed before Jake properly woke up.

'I see you've shared the pyjamas,' went on Mrs Morgan chattily, and Helen realised she thought that Jake must be wearing the trousers. So instead of disabusing her, Helen just smiled and waited for her to go.

But it soon became obvious that Mrs Morgan was in no hurry to leave, and she fussed about unnecessarily, drawing back the curtains and tidying the things on the dressing table until Helen felt she could scream.

With an effort she applied herself to her tea, drinking the hot liquid slowly, but of course the constant sound of activity in the room eventually disturbed Jake and he opened his eyes, a frown marring his forehead for a brief moment when he saw Helen. Then a strange smile slid over his face before his eyes travelled on round the room to encounter those of Mrs Morgan.

'Ah, you're awake at last!' she exclaimed, smiling with approval. 'I've brought you both a tray of tea, and your wife says you'd like bacon and eggs for breakfast, is that right?'

Jake levered himself up on his elbows. To Helen, seeing him like this, relaxed and drowsy-eyed, his hair tousled and the shadow of a night's beard on his chin, it was a disturbing experience, and she was intensely conscious of the nearness of his warm body beneath the covers.

Jake smiled at the Welsh woman and said: 'That sounds exactly what I need, Mrs Morgan. If it's not too much trouble.'

'Of course it's no trouble.' Mrs Morgan folded her arms across her ample bosom. 'Did you sleep comfortably?'

Jake flicked a glance in Helen's direction, but she was leaning over to replace her empty cup on the tray and therefore avoided his questioning gaze. He made some suitable reply to Mrs

Morgan, and then there was a moment's awkward silence while Mrs Morgan waited, apparently for either of them to say something else. When no further comment seemed forthcoming, the older woman was forced to walk reluctantly towards the door.

'I'll have the meal ready in half an hour. Will that suit you both?'

Helen hesitated. 'That will be lovely, but nothing for me, thank you, Mrs Morgan. I usually have a slice of toast—'

'And nothing else?' Mrs Morgan was scandalised. 'And you so slim? You need a good breakfast, that's what I always say.'

'Really, Mrs Morgan, I'm not hungry.' Helen could not have faced a cooked breakfast this morning for anything.

The woman made an impatient gesture. 'Oh, well, if you insist. But I'll do you plenty of toast, and there's some home-made marmalade to go with it.'

'Lovely!' Helen managed another smile, and to her relief Mrs Morgan took it as dismissal. She went out, closing the door behind her, and Helen heaved a sigh before turning as though to get out of bed.

'Wait!' Jake caught her wrist, preventing her from sliding out of the bed. 'What's the hurry? It smells damn cold out there!'

'I should have been up before you woke up if

Mrs Morgan hadn't persisted in hanging about!' Helen replied heatedly.

Jake retained his hold on her wrist, lying back on his pillows with indolent grace. 'So what kept you?'

Helen flushed. 'Mrs Morgan thought we were sharing the pyjamas. If I'd got out of bed she would have seen that we weren't.'

Jake half smiled. 'And that would have embarrassed Mrs Morgan? I somehow don't think so.'

Helen pursed her lips. 'It would have embarrassed me!' she retorted shortly. 'Now will you please let go of my wrist?'

Jake ignored her plea, his eyes narrowing thoughtfully. 'This is quite a novel situation, isn't it? Our being in bed together for the first time after three years of marriage.'

Helen glared angrily at him, struggling to free herself without result. 'I shouldn't have thought it would be much of a novelty for you!' she cried scornfully.

'No?' Jake's eyes glittered at the contempt in her voice.

'No.' Helen attempted to prise his fingers from her wrist. 'Let me go!'

'I want to know why you think it shouldn't be a novelty for me,' he stated, his voice cold and determined.

Helen stared at him impotently, wishing she had never made any reply to his comment. She invariably said the wrong thing. 'Jake, please, you're hurting me! We don't have that long. Mrs Morgan said breakfast would be ready in half an hour—'

'To hell with Mrs Morgan!' Jake propped himself up on one elbow and forced her back against her pillows by increasing the pressure on her wrist. 'Well?' he asked harshly. 'Aren't you going to tell me what that not so innocent little mind of yours has dreamed up about me now?'

Helen moved her head from side to side. 'You—you beast!' Her breast heaved. 'I—I'll scream!'

'You could. But you won't. Imagine what construction Mrs Morgan would put on it if you did.'

Helen stared at him helplessly. 'Jake, please!' she begged. 'Let me go! This is—this is—' Her voice trailed away weakly. She was overwhelmingly conscious of his nearness, and the intimacy of this situation, and while she told herself she wanted to escape from him, part of her resisted such a sane and sensible solution.

Jake's gaze raked her mobile face ruthlessly, and then his lips twisted. 'This is—what?' he demanded coldly. 'Reckless? Dangerous, perhaps?' He uttered a short mirthless laugh. 'Oh, Helen, who do you think you're kidding? Do you honestly imagine I don't know what goes on inside that beautiful head? Do you think I wasn't aware of how you felt last night when I comforted you in the car park of the hotel?' His tone was contemptuous now. 'Do you think I don't know women well enough to know when they become interested in a man? All this uncharacteristic indignation—this assumed anger! It's all an act! Designed for one purpose and one purpose only: to make me aware of you as you appear to be aware of me!'

Helen was horrified. 'How dare you!' she gasped. 'How dare you suggest such a thing!' She was beside herself with anger. 'Don't judge everybody by your standards!'

'Why not?' Jake's smouldering gaze moved lazily over her face and down her neck, lingering on the parting lapels of the enormous pyjama jacket. 'Isn't it the truth?'

Helen's whole body suffused with colour at that devastating appraisal, and then abruptly, he released her, sliding out of bed himself and pulling on his suede trousers over his trunk-like underwear, which was all he had worn to sleep in.

Helen lay where he had left her, one arm raised protectively to shade her eyes, unwillingly aware that tears of frustration and humiliation were not far away. No matter how she might protest, she had to admit to herself that in part he was right. She was aware of him now in a way she had hitherto not been aware of any man, and the knowledge was eating her up with—*jealousy*!' She caught her breath. The dreadful meaning of that word was not lost on her and she turned on to her stomach, burying her face in the pillow so that Jake should not see her shame.

Jake finished dressing and ran a practised hand over his jawline. 'I need a shave,' he remarked matter-of-factly, and Helen hated him anew for being able to dismiss what had happened so summarily. But then his emotions had not been involved, and a pain crawled in her stomach when she thought that he was capable of sleeping in the same bed as herself without so much as attempting a pass at her. It was doubly humiliating when she considered the sensual nature she had credited him with. Was she so unattractive to him that he could ignore the fact that she was flesh and blood like any other woman?

'I hesitate to remind you, but Mrs Morgan did state half an hour,' Jake was saying now, standing beside the bed, looking down on her half buried beneath the covers. 'I thought you wanted to get up.'

'Go away!' Helen's voice was muffled and indistinct.

'All right.' Jake sounded indifferent. 'I was going to allow you to use the bathroom first.'

'Go to hell!'

Helen burrowed deeper into the pillows, and with a shrug of his broad shoulders, Jake turned and walked lazily towards the door.

'By the way,' he remarked, as he put out a hand

to take the handle, 'you'd better pour yourself a second cup of tea in *my* cup or Mrs Morgan will consider you a rather indifferent wife!'

One of Helen's pillows hit the door as it closed behind him and she knelt up in the bed, her lips pressed together mutinously. He had to have the last word, she thought resentfully, and then climbed hastily off the bed, tugging on her clothes. She had no desire for him to walk back in while she was dressing.

When he did come back she was combing her hair at the mirror and he came to stand behind her, smoothing his own hair with a careless hand. He had not shaved and the shadow on his jawline was more pronounced. He smoothed a hand down his sideburns, and then said:

'You'd better hurry. We don't have a lot of time.'

Helen turned abruptly and walked to the door, and with a careless movement of his shoulders Jake walked to the bed and began tugging the covers back into some kind of order. Helen's last antics on the bed had loosened all the sheets and blankets, and they were strewn in careless disorder.

Helen frowned as she opened the door, and Jake remarked mockingly: 'I should hate to leave the wrong impression.'

Helen went out seething, sure there was no way of getting under his skin.

Jake ate an enormous breakfast, watched by Helen and Mrs Morgan with varying degrees of solicitude. To Helen, choking on coffee and a slice of toast, it was nauseating to watch him plough his way through fruit juice, cereal, bacon, eggs, sausages and tomatoes, toast and marmalade and tea, and she wondered whether she would ever be able to achieve his calm indifference again. Nothing seemed to perturb him more than momentarily, and certainly this morning the lines of weariness were gone from his eyes, leaving his face dark and alert and attractive.

Mr Morgan appeared from the barn soon after the meal and after saying goodbye to Mrs Morgan they all went down the track to the road.

'I've asked my boy David to come down with the tractor,' Mr Morgan said, as they squelched through mud which would soon dry in the unexpected sunshine. 'I shouldn't think you'll have any more difficulty now that it's fine and light.'

Jake shook his head. 'I very much appreciate all you and your wife have done for us,' he said warmly. 'I'm sure our weekend couldn't have got off to a better start, eh, Helen?'

'Oh—oh, yes!' The words stuck in Helen's throat, but she managed to infuse enthusiasm into them.

Jake's eyes flickered over her, and she quickly looked away, wishing with all her heart she had not agreed to spend this weekend with him.

David Morgan soon brought the Ferrari out of the ditch and it stood there in the sunlight, muddy but magnificent.

'That's some car, boyo,' remarked Mr Morgan, looking inside with interest. He smiled at Jake. 'I bet you can make it go.'

Jake grinned. 'On these roads? Hardly.'

'Was that how you ended up in the ditch last night?'

Jake hesitated. 'Sort of,' he agreed lazily, glancing meaningfully at Helen. 'Well, we must go.'

Mr Morgan refused to accept anything from Jake for their night's lodging, and Jake climbed into the car, putting his wallet away reluctantly. Then the powerful engine roared to life, and after more waving they drove off.

Helen relaxed in her seat feeling suddenly decidedly weak. Altogether the incident had been rather exhausting.

Jake did not speak as he turned off on the road to Llandranog and Helen began to feel apprehensive about the coming ordeal. What if the Ndanas were not her kind of people? What if she couldn't get on with them? What if Jake did do as Jennifer had suggested and disappeared with the Ambassador leaving Helen to entertain his wife? What would they have to talk about?

But she showed none of her anxieties to Jake,

who seemed absorbed with his own thoughts. Mrs Morgan had dried and brushed their coats so that there was no sign of the muddy, bedraggled garments they had seemed the night before, and only the fact that Jake needed a shave and Helen wore no make-up revealed that they had spent the night at the farm.

Presently they ran into a small village, nestling confidingly in the valley, and Helen pointed out the signpost.

'Well, as this is Llandranog, the cottage should be this way,' remarked Jake, following the first turn left out of the village.

It was quite a bright morning now, the sun banishing the clouds and leaving a clear expanse of blue, and although the wind was cold it was bracing. In no time at all, Jake was turning between a wrought iron gateway and approaching a small house, overhung with ivy and climbing plants that somehow managed to survive the wild winds off the mountains. Running beside the house was a narrow stream, the water cascading noisily over silvery stones, and providing a constant backcloth to the other sounds of everyday living.

'Oh, it's beautiful!' exclaimed Helen impulsively, and Jake glanced at her mockingly.

'How many bedrooms do you suppose there are?' he queried lazily, and Helen's cheeks suffused with colour.

'Do you mean—will they think—?' Helen stopped, aghast.

Jake's eyes hardened. 'And if they do? What of it? Nothing happened last night, and you weren't too uncomfortable at six o'clock this morning when I was woken by the dogs barking!'

Helen slid abruptly out of the car, and as she did so the door of the house opened, and Ndana and his wife appeared. Their dark faces were warm and welcoming and Helen's earlier misgivings were instantly dispersed.

'So you've arrived at last, man!' Ndana was saying, grinning broadly, coming forward to shake Jake's hand as he too got out of the car. 'We were beginning to have our doubts.'

Jake shook hands with Ndana warmly, punching his shoulder in a manner which left Helen in no doubt that these two knew one another far better than it was publicly stated. 'What a journey, Lucien!' Jake was saying ironically. 'God! Couldn't you and Rose have found yourselves a hideaway in Notting Hill or St John's Wood?'

Lucien Ndana chuckled, 'Now, Jake, you know we like to get back to the wilds whenever we can!'

Jake burst out laughing and Rose Ndana joined in. For a moment, Helen felt rather isolated. Jake obviously knew Lucien's wife as well, and she knew him, judging by the mischievous glances she was casting in his direction. But as she was also obviously pregnant, her darting glances were merely teasing.

Lucien looked beyond Jake at that moment and smiled at Helen and as though remembering his wife, Jake drew Helen forward, introducing her with casual expertise.

Lucien studied Helen for a long moment, and then he said: 'She's beautiful, Jake. But that's no surprise—you never chose anything but the best!' He released Helen's hand reluctantly. 'I hope you're going to enjoy yourself this weekend, Helen. We promise not to talk business for more than fifty per cent of the time!'

Helen managed a smile. 'I'm sure I'm going to love it,' she said enthusiastically. 'I like your house. It's charming!'

Rose Ndana said little, but she smiled a lot, and when they all walked into the house, entering a flower-filled hallway that was panelled in rich mahogany, she suggested that she showed Helen their room while Lucien got Jake a drink.

Jake looked at Helen for verification, and she nodded slightly. 'I think that's a good idea,' she said. 'Jake can get the cases later.'

'Oh, Mujari will get them,' replied Rose calmly, leading the way up a carved wooden staircase, and glancing round Helen saw Jake handing his keys to an enormous black man dressed in casual clothes over which he wore a capacious white apron. Rose, following the trend of Helen's thoughts, said: 'Mujari does everything around here. He's marvellous! And he's also quite useful as a bodyguard!'

Helen raised startled eyebrows. 'Your husband needs a bodyguard?'

Rose shrugged. She was smaller than Helen, and slimmer too, Helen judged, when she was not pregnant, and her shoulders were very narrow. 'All statesmen need bodyguards in my country,' she said quietly. 'Not that they are always effective, of course. Assassins choose their moments.'

Helen was amazed. 'How frightening!'

'One becomes accustomed to such things,' replied Rose simply. 'Now—here is your room. Do you like it?'

Helen's heart palpitated alarmingly as Rose thrust open a door near the head of the stairs and indicated that Helen should precede her inside. It was a large room, bright and attractive, the furniture light oak, the curtains and bedcoverings in a delicious shade of apricot. There were twin beds.

Helen heaved a tremulous sigh. 'It—it's lovely!' she said at last.

Rose smiled in a pleased way. 'I'm glad you like it. Now—come and met the children!'

Helen's lips parted. Rose scarcely looked old enough to have a family. 'You have children?'

'Yes. Didn't Jake tell you? Three. . .and of course. . .' She smiled down meaningfully at her swollen stomach.

Helen felt her colour rising. 'No—no, Jake didn't tell me. Where are they?'

'They're in the nursery with Lisa, our nanny. Come, I'll introduce you.'

Rose led the way down the panelled hall of the landing and entered a room at the far end. Helen following her found herself in a gaily decorated nursery where a slim red-haired girl was doing her best to keep three excited infants under control.

'Come in, Helen,' said Rose smilingly. 'This is Lisa. Lisa, this is Mrs Howard, Jake Howard's wife.'

Lisa straightened to face Helen. She was about Helen's height, but slimmer, with narrow shoulders and hips. Two of the children still clung to her hands, one of whom was no more than ten or eleven months and stood on wobbling legs, while the other was a boy of perhaps three. The third child, a girl of four or five, had run to her mother when Rose entered the room.

'How do you do?' she murmured politely, but there was no welcome in her eyes. On the contrary, she was regarding Helen in a wholly hostile manner, and Helen couldn't immediately understand why.

Rose seemed unaware of the tension in the atmosphere and said: 'What do you think of my babies?' She looked down at the little girl clinging to her skirt. 'This is Ruth, and that's Joseph with Lisa. The baby is called James.'

She smiled and bent to pick up her youngest child.
'Hello, darling! Are you being a good boy
for Lisa?'

Helen tried to retain her composure under the
nanny's critical gaze. 'They're beautiful children,' she said, and they were—black and chubby
and wholly adorable.

Rose looked complacent. 'Yes, they are, aren't
they? Lucien and I are very proud of them. And
Lisa is a treasure, of course.'

'I'm sure she must be.' Helen wet her dry lips.
'Have you been with Mrs Ndana long, Lisa?'

Lisa shrugged. 'Two years,' she said indifferently.

'Since we came to England,' explained Rose.
'I expect Lisa will be returning to Tsaba with us
when we eventually go back, won't you, Lisa?'

Lisa looked at her employer and her expression
changed. 'I'd like to hope so,' she said warmly.

Rose touched her shoulder gently, and then
turned. 'Well, we must go. The men will be
wondering where we are.'

It was only as they were descending the stairs
that Helen remembered something Rose had said.
When she had introduced Helen to Lisa she had
called her *Mrs* Howard, and then she had gone
on to say that Helen was *Jake* Howard's wife.
Almost as though Lisa knew Jake—as Jake!

Helen felt a sinking feeling in the pit of her
stomach. Did Lisa know her husband? Did she

know him well? And as it was obvious that Jake had visited the Ndanas many times before, why had he brought her with him this time?

CHAPTER SEVEN

DOWNSTAIRS, the men were lounging before the fire in the living room, glasses of beer in their hands, talking amicably. They both stood up as Helen and Rose entered the room, but Helen avoided her husband's eyes, looking instead at Lucien, asking him about the history of the house saying how much she liked it.

Lucien was reassuringly attentive, only too willing to tell her all about the place and how it had been converted from an old mill in the nineteenth century. Helen was interested, but it was difficult to prevent her mind from probing Jake's involvement with the Ndanas, and why he should have chosen to bring her here this weekend. Contrary to Jennifer's beliefs he seemed to have no reason for maintaining a comfortable husband-and-wife relationship with these people who obviously knew him so well, and he had never previously shown any desire to introduce her to his friends other than at the formal dinner parties held at their house in Kersland Square. So why had she been invited? Because his relationship with the Ndanas' nanny, Lisa, was getting out of hand? Because, as with his other women, she was asking too much of him?

Helen's lips tightened, and she flicked a glance in Jake's direction. He was not looking at her at that moment and she surveyed him frustratedly. Why did he have to have that disturbing magnetism that drew all women to him like moths round a flame? What was there about a man who had striven ruthlessly all his life to reach the top and who had succeeded by his own efforts, who had never had a lesson in diplomacy in his life, and who rode roughshod over anyone who got in his way that convinced every woman he met that she was the one who had the necessary attributes to tame him?

Helen absently accepted a cigarette from Lucien and bent her head to his lighter. Inhaling deeply, she forced herself to concentrate on what he was saying. But she was constantly aware of Jake's dark head bent towards Rose's, and the way he seemed to be giving his whole attention to what she was saying. *What was she saying?* The desire to know was eating Helen up, and she realised with a sense of dismay that she was jealous, intensely so.

Desperately she turned back to Lucien, and said: 'Could we look around outside? I'd love a walk in the sunshine. Is the old mill wheel still there?'

Lucien nodded. 'Yes, it's still there,' he agreed

mildly. 'But rather dilapidated, I'm afraid. But if you'd like a walk, we can all go. Hey, Jake, want to stretch your legs?'

'I don't mind.' Jake looked across at them easily. 'How about you, Rose?'

Rose patted her stomach. 'I don't somehow think so,' she replied regretfully. 'I think I'll just sit by the fire until lunchtime.'

Jake thrust his hands deep into the pockets of his trousers. 'Then perhaps I'll stay and keep Rose company,' he remarked quietly. Helen knew he was looking at her, but she refused to look at him and he gave a casual shrug of his shoulders. 'Do you want me to stay, Rose?'

Rose smiled, a warm intimate smile. 'I shouldn't keep you from your lovely wife,' she demurred.

Jake's expression hardened. 'Don't let it worry you,' he remarked dryly. 'Helen can do very well without my company.'

Helen looked at him then and saw the sardonic glint in his eyes. 'How right you are!' she retorted pleasantly, and had the satisfaction of seeing his momentary impatience with her insolence.

Lucien Ndana seemed to see nothing wrong, however, and after Helen had collected her coat they went out into the blustery autumn sunshine. And despite her conviction that she would not do so, Helen did enjoy herself. Lucien was a stimulating companion, and interspersed with the history of the mill house he told her a little of his own country, Tsaba, in central Africa. To Helen their tribal customs were fascinating and they were engrossed in a discussion of African culture when they returned to the house.

Lunch was being served by Mujari, and he was introduced to Helen almost as a member of the family. The children did not eat with their parents and consequently there was just the four of them. Fortunately, Lucien did most of the talking, but although Jake made some comment to Rose he did not look in Helen's direction and she told herself she was glad.

After lunch the men retired to Lucien's study to discuss the new project and as Rose explained that she usually rested after the meal Helen was left to her own devices. Putting on her coat again, she walked down to the village, going into the village store and buying some sweets for the children. Then she walked slowly back, arriving just as Rose was in the process of carrying a tray of tea into the living room.

Helen smiled, 'Did you enjoy your rest?'

Rose smiled in return. 'Thank you, yes. I'm sorry I had to leave you alone so long. Where have you been?'

Helen dropped the packet of sweets on the low table in front of the fire. 'I went to the village store. These are some sweets for Ruth, Joseph, and James.'

'How kind!' Rose patted the seat on the couch beside her. 'Come and sit down. We haven't had much chance to talk yet. Tell me, when are you and Jake thinking of starting a family?'

Helen blushed scarlet. 'Oh—well, we—haven't really thought—about it,' she stammered awkwardly.

Rose frowned. 'But you have been married three years, haven't you? Don't you want a family?'

Helen wetted her dry lips with her tongue. 'Of—of course I do,' she murmured swiftly. 'It's just—well, not convenient, right now.'

'Why?' Rose was unashamedly curious.

Helen shook her head helplessly. What could she say? She accepted the tea Rose handed to her and wondered with a sense of hysterical mirth what the other girl would say if she knew the truth about their marriage. Or perhaps she did know, and she was merely probing Helen's reactions.

But somehow Helen didn't think so. Rose wasn't that kind of woman. To her, having children was the most natural thing in the world and being married without them was an alien state.

The sound of voices in the hall relieved the situation and Helen was inordinately glad when Jake and Lucien came into the room, Lucien's eyes lighting up when he saw the tray of tea and scones.

'Just in time, I see,' he observed cheerfully. 'Come on, Jake, take a scone. They're Mujari's speciality, believe it or not!'

Jake came to take the armchair near Helen accepting a scone and a cup of tea with lazy complacency. He was obviously at home with the Ndanas despite the fact that he had never actually been here before.

Lucien took the armchair opposite and said: 'I've suggested to Jake that he should come out to Tsaba with me next month when I go back for the Assembly.'

Helen's heart plunged. Was Jake planning to go away again?

Rose sipped her tea delicately. 'And how long do you plan to be away, Lucien? I don't want you in Tsaba when the baby is born.'

Lucien grinned. 'Now, Rose, you know the baby's not due for another three months. I'll be back long before then.'

Rose grimaced at Helen. 'These men!' she exclaimed. 'Always going off somewhere! They don't care about their wives leading lonely uninteresting lives without them!'

Helen agreed privately, but she didn't say so and Jake regarded her intently, forcing her to meet his gaze. 'Well?' he demanded. 'Haven't you anything to say, Helen?'

Helen raised her dark eyebrows. 'I'm sure it must be important if you have to go to Tsaba,' she remarked, with admirable composure considering she was a mass of angry nerves and resentments inside. 'When do you expect to leave?'

Lucien chuckled delightedly. 'You see!' he exclaimed, looking at Rose. 'You see how well trained Helen is! She doesn't even make an objection even though her husband is about to take a six weeks' trip to Central Africa! How about that?'

Helen coloured. Was that how her reaction had seemed? The obedient acquiescence of a well-trained household pet! She pressed her lips together, staring down at the cup of tea in her hands. She felt that Jake had humiliated her once again even though he had said nothing.

Rose herself looked rather indignant. 'Helen doesn't have three children to care for, Lucien. She's a free agent. She can come and go as she pleases, have whatever friends she likes.'

Lucien looked at her reproachfully. 'Lisa is perfectly capable of caring for the children. You don't have to stay home all the time.'

Rose sniffed. 'And where can I go? How can I wear pretty clothes looking like this!'

Lucien shook his head. 'Now, Rose,' he said again, and she hunched her shoulders, silencing any further protest she might have been tempted to make.

Helen replaced her tea cup on the tray, a rising sense of injustice swelling up inside her. She could understand Rose's resentment, her feeling of living apart from her husband's life. Helen had known that same feeling.

An awkward silence had fallen and Helen rose determinedly to her feet. 'Would it be all right if I took a bath?' she inquired of Rose, and the dark girl was glad to change the subject.

'Of course,' she said. 'Mujari has put your cases in your room. You know where it is.'

'Yes.' Helen managed a slight smile, and then walked quickly out of the room. It was a relief to escape from Jake's presence and she lingered in the deep bath she had run herself, luxuriating in its perfumed softness.

Eventually, of course, she had to come out, and by this time it was almost dark outside and the early autumn evening was drawing in. Rose had said dinner was usually served about eight after she and Lucien had spent an hour with the children, so she had plenty of time. Donning only a towelling robe, she returned to the bedroom, but when she entered she found the lamps lit and Jake lounging lazily on one of the beds.

Her colour deepened when she saw him and she automatically tightened her robe about her as she closed the door.

'You've taken long enough,' he commented dourly, his dark eyes brooding.

Helen folded her towel and hung it casually over the hand basin in the corner of the room. 'I'm sorry,' she said, coolly and politely. 'I didn't know you were waiting to use the bathroom.'

'There are two bathrooms. If I'd wanted to use the bathroom I'd have used the other,' replied Jake shortly. 'No, I've been waiting to speak to you—privately.'

'Oh yes?' Helen picked up her brush and began brushing her heavy swathe of hair.

Her indifferent action must have irritated him, for he said grimly: 'Damn you, yes! I want to know what's got into you since we arrived here.' He swung his legs to the ground and sat up. 'Don't tell me it's this proposed trip to Africa! You were acting strangely long before that came up. Besides, you must have guessed that was on the cards in any case.'

Helen controlled the impulse to throw the hairbrush at him. He sat there on the bed calmly asking her why she was behaving strangely, when he must know that she had every reason to be suspicious of his motives for bringing her here.

'Tell me something first,' she said tautly. 'Why did you insist on bringing me here? I thought at first it was to impress the Ndanas, but it's obvious you don't need to impress them. So why was I brought here? Protection, perhaps?'

Jake uttered an angry ejaculation, and getting to his feet he strode across to her, swinging her round to face him, the hairbrush still clutched in her hand.

'What do you mean by that?' he demanded

fiercely. 'Why should I need protection?'

Helen was frightened, but she managed to retain her composure, outwardly at least although her voice was slightly uneven. 'You tell me!'

'I haven't the faintest idea what you're talking about!' Jake replied coldly.

'Haven't you?' Helen's voice trembled a little now. 'I suppose you're going to deny that you know the Ndanas' nanny, Lisa.'

Jake frowned deeply. 'Lisa? Lisa Harding? No, of course I'm not going to deny I know her.'

Helen shook her head. 'Oh, no, of course not. I should have realised you would be prepared for that one. It would be stupid to deny knowing someone in this household, wouldn't it?'

'Helen, for God's sake, get to the point!'

Helen straightened her shoulders. 'The girl hates me,' she said distinctly. 'When I met her this morning it was obvious. She really hates me. And there could be only one explanation for that—'

'Oh, God!' Jake caught her shoulders through the towelling material of her robe. 'All right, all right, I know Lisa. I admit I've taken her out a couple of times, but that was ages ago. In actual fact I got her this job with the Ndanas. And I've certainly never taken any interest in her since then!'

'Do you expect me to believe that?' Helen's breathing was constricted. 'You—you've obviously visited the Ndanas a lot. And this is the first time I've been with you. . .'

Jake raised his eyes heavenward. 'Look, Helen, Lisa Harding means absolutely nothing to me. Why should I lie about it? And you don't really give a damn anyway. You're just using this as a lever so that I won't object about your involvement with that prig Mannering!'

Helen held up her head. 'I am not involved with Keith Mannering,' she denied hotly.

'Aren't you?' Jake's expression was ironic. 'Do you mean to tell me he's never held you in his arms—never kissed you?'

'Of course not.' Helen's cheeks burned.

'Then how do you hold him on a thread? What does he get out of the situation?'

Helen seethed, her anger displacing her fear of him. 'It may interest you to know that there are relationships between a man and a woman that do not rely on sex as the intermediary!'

Jake's eyes hardened. 'Indeed? A purely intellectual association, I suppose.'

'You could call it that!'

'So what does Mannering get out of such an association?'

Helen raised her eyebrows. 'He doesn't get anything—at least nothing tangible. We just share opinions—'

'Instead of beds, is that it?' Jake's eyes glinted, dangerously.

Helen's cheeks burned. 'You have to reduce everything to the physical, haven't you?' she cried angrily. 'You can't visualise sharing ideas with a member of the opposite sex, can you? You think only men have the prerogative to discuss things intelligently.'

'Oh, no, I don't think that,' said Jake grimly. 'But I know Mannering, and I'm damned sure he isn't as happy with your platonic relationship as you appear to be. What is it with you, Helen? What's missing from that exquisite body of yours that you can't appreciate a normal healthy relationship?'

Helen caught her breath on a sob. 'Is that what you call your association with women like Lisa Harding?' she demanded disgustedly. 'Normal healthy relationships?'

Jake looked down at her, his lips twisting contemptuously. Then his eyes darkened as they dropped lower, lingering on the cleft between her breasts, just visible above the parting neckline of the robe. His fingers which had been gripping her shoulders tightened fractionally.

'I've taken a lot from you,' he murmured huskily.

Helen swallowed with difficulty. 'You're hurting me,' she said, her voice scarcely above a whisper.

'Am I?' His eyes narrowed, and Helen felt

the bones in her lower limbs dissolving beneath his gaze.

'Jake, *please*,' she murmured breathlessly.

Jake moved closer to her, the hardness of his body touching hers. 'You're trembling,' he said, bending his head and putting his mouth lingeringly against the side of her neck. 'I can stop that.' And then his mouth was on hers and her lips were parting almost without volition.

His kiss, which started so gently, became urgent, passionate, destroying all her inexperienced illusions of what a kiss should be. Jake was an expert when it came to arousing a woman, and his hands slid possessively down her back to her hips, pressing her closer against him, making her wholly aware of his own needs.

Helen wanted to resist him. She would have liked to have escaped from his arms and shown him that she could not be influenced in this way. But it was useless to pretend. The warmth of his lean muscular body, the disturbing hunger of his mouth, the probing caress of his hands, all left her weak and clinging to him, despising herself even while her arms slid compulsively round his neck, her fingers sliding through the thick vitality of his hair. She lost all count of time and place, his love-making seducing her to a state of mind where nothing mattered but him, his urgent need of her. She wanted him, too, her body ached for his, and when he swung her up into his arms and carried her to the bed she felt an overpowering sense of achievement.

Her eyes were closed, but she opened them as he laid her on the bed, and she saw something that struck a shaft of fear through her system. His eyes were no longer warm and disturbing, but hard and cold, and completely alien. Helen felt a terrible wave of degradation sweep over her and she wrapped the towelling robe protectively about her, wanting to close her eyes against the accusation in his.

'Now tell me!' he demanded violently straightening. 'Mannering has never touched you?'

Helen turned her head from side to side, shivering in spite of the heat of her body. He hasn't!' she whispered tormentedly. 'No one has!'

Jake stared at her for a long considering moment. 'What are you trying to make me do?' he asked savagely. 'Prove it?'

Helen's lips parted. 'I don't tell lies, Jake,' she said tremulously.

'Oh, God!'

Jake smote a hand to his forehead and without another word he turned and strode out of the room.

Helen lay on the bed in a kind of agonised stupor, dreading the moment when Jake must return to get changed for dinner. Her mind raced incoherently through the implications of what had happened, but it was impossible to achieve a sense of reality in it all. She felt completely drained of all energy, the languor which his love-making had aroused in her still uppermost in her feelings.

Eventually, she knew she would have to stir herself. The last thing she wanted was for Jake to return and imagine she was lying there waiting for him. He might despise her, but he could not despise her as much as she despised herself.

She, Helen Forsythe, who had always felt contempt for women who threw themselves at men who didn't want them, had proved herself no better than the rest.

Determinedly, she slid off the bed. She would not lie there soaking herself in self-pity. The very last thing Jake would expect from her was a fight, but he was going to get one. She would not make matters worse by giving him any reason to think she reproached him for what had happened. She would act as though the last half hour had never occurred, and somehow recover the shattered illusion of detachment.

In consequence, she took especial pains with her make-up, smoothing pale green eye shadow on to her lids, darkening the already dark lashes, adding a colourless lustre to her lips. Then she took out the dress she was going to wear, a long wine-coloured velvet gown that had a low dipping neck-line and modestly full long sleeves. She had never worn the gown before, and it complemented her extreme fairness in a way that gave an added touch of fragility to her appearance. She wore the hoops of gold in her ears, and a medallion about her neck that fell enticingly into the hollow between her breasts.

When she surveyed her appearance before going downstairs she knew she had never looked lovelier, and because of this she was able to appear confident when actually she was anything but.

Jake had still not returned to their room and she went downstairs tentatively, dreading the encounter that was to come and yet longing for him to see her.

However, when she entered the living room she found only Lisa Harding there, dressed formally in a green caftan that went well with her cap of red hair. She looked surprised to see Helen, and her lashes veiled the expression in her eyes.

But Helen was determined to act naturally, and she greeted the girl pleasantly and said: 'Where are the others?'

Lisa folded her hands together, hostility still evident in her withdrawn manner. 'Everyone else is with the children,' she replied politely. 'My employers usually spend this time of day with their sons and daughter, and your husband invariably finds the time to join them. He's very fond of children.'

Helen inclined her head. 'I see,' she murmured, glancing round the room in an effort to remain calm. 'I didn't realise. . .'

Lisa's nostrils flared. 'Can I offer you a drink? I'm sure Mrs Ndana would approve.'

Helen hesitated. 'Why—yes, thank you. Sherry would be fine.'

'Sweet or dry?'

'Dry, please.' Helen bit her lower lip. 'Do you like working for the Ndanas?'

Lisa poured the sherry without interest and handed the glass indifferently to Helen. 'Very much,' she said. 'Jake got me the job.'

Helen stiffened slightly but not perceptibly. 'Yes. Yes, he told me,' she said.

'Did he?' Lisa looked sceptical. 'I've known Jake for a number of years. I was born in Leeds, you see. We met at a party there about ten years ago.'

'As long as that?' Helen sounded surprised. After all, ten years ago she herself would have been only fifteen.

'Yes.' Lisa's lips twisted. 'I know his mother too.'

Helen sipped her sherry. 'This is exceptionally good sherry, and at just the right temperature.'

Lisa's lips tightened. 'Of course. You'd be an expert on such things.'

Helen was shocked at the contempt in the girl's voice, but she managed to hide her own feelings.

'Would I?' she said now, without rancour.

Lisa shrugged her thin shoulders. 'Tell me, Mrs Howard,' she said disparagingly, 'don't you ever get bored?'

Helen looked up. 'Bored? Why should I get bored?'

Lisa shrugged again. 'Jake being away such a lot—leaving you alone. Don't you ever feel like getting a job of some kind?'

Helen's brows drew together in a slight frown. 'I see. Well, yes, I suppose sometimes I do get bored. But not generally speaking. I read a lot— I go to the theatre—to art exhibitions! My time is quite adequately filled, I think.'

Lisa clicked her tongue. 'All the women Jake had to choose from, and he chose a lily of the field like you!'

Helen traced the rim of her glass with her finger. 'I think you're becoming rather insolent, Miss Harding,' she said carefully.

Lisa sniffed. 'I don't care what you think. Jake should have had more sense. His mother agrees with me, too.'

'Does she?' Helen raised her dark eyebrows. 'But then mothers can't choose their sons' wives, can they? You're overlooking the fact that Jake is a very determined man. I somehow can't see him doing anything he didn't want to do, can you?'

Lisa flushed. 'It was your background he wanted—*not you!*'

Helen forced a sardonic smile. 'That may have been true once, Lisa,' she said deliberately, 'but do you honestly think it's true now?' The slightly mocking lift of her lips was sufficient to make the other girl clench her fists angrily, and Helen knew she had chosen exactly the right way to demolish Lisa's attack. She ran a questing hand down over her hips, emphasising the slender curve of her thighs. 'Tell me,' she went on lazily, 'do you think this material suits me?'

Lisa uttered an ugly expletive and disappeared out of the door, and Helen heaved a shaking sigh of relief. At least in that little skirmish she had come out the victor.

Lucien and Rose appeared a few minutes later, nodding approvingly when they saw she had a drink. 'Lisa gave it to me,' said Helen, raising the glass. 'Are the children settled in for the night?'

Lucien grinned. 'Oh, Lisa will settle them down. She always has the last word.'

'Does she?' Helen bent her head thoughtfully, and just at that moment Jake came into the room.

He had bathed and shaved and changed into a dark lounge suit, the trousers of which fitted the muscular length of his legs closely. He was wearing a pale blue shirt and matching tie, and his dark hair was smooth and attractively curling at his collar. He really was the most disturbingly masculine being, Helen thought shakenly, aware that her stomach was behaving most peculiarly, and a lingering ache made itself apparent.

Jake's gaze slid over his wife almost indifferently, and yet, from time to time during the course of the meal, Helen became conscious of him staring at her, a curious brooding expression in his eyes. She felt herself dreading the moment when they would retire for the night and be alone again. She didn't think she could bear any more of his contempt.

Lisa did not join them for dinner, and Rose explained that although they had invited her she had preferred to eat her meal in her room. Helen was relieved. Lisa's antipathy was something she could do without.

After dinner the men excused themselves on the pretext of playing a game of chess in Lucien's study, and Helen was again left with Rose. But fortunately the television took Rose's interest and prevented her asking any more personal questions.

The evening dragged by slowly, Helen finding herself more and more uneasy. Eventually, after Mujari had brought them a tray of coffee and sandwiches about ten o'clock, she excused herself, and Rose seemed more than willing to retire as well.

'These men!' she said, shaking her head. 'They don't care about us at all.' But she laughed as she said it and Helen knew she was not serious.

In the bedroom, after a brief sojourn in the bathroom, Helen put on her nightgown and climbed into bed. It had been a strange day and she felt sure she would not sleep, and she was right.

Her mind buzzed with thoughts of Jake's coming trip to Tsaba, of her conversation with Lisa Harding, of Jake's brooding manner all evening, and most important of all, his behaviour earlier on in this bedroom. Or perhaps she had been responsible for that, she thought, sighing. She had goaded him and he had retaliated in a way that had proved to her beyond any doubt that she was no longer indifferent to him.

She deliberately turned on to her stomach and tried to put all thoughts of him out of her mind, but it was practically impossible. The sounds of the night came to her: the rustling of the wind through the trees outside, the tumbling sound of the brook, the cry of a night bird. And presently she heard doors opening and shutting and realised that Jake and Lucien were coming to bed.

Immediately she lay completely still, and when their bedroom door opened she pretended to breathe deeply so that he would think she was asleep.

But Jake put on the lamp between the beds and opening an eye she saw him beginning to take off his clothes. Closing her eyes tightly again, she waited for him to finish and turn out the light and get into his own bed.

Eventually he did turn out the light, but instead of going to his own bed he came to hers, and she was conscious of him standing there in the darkness, looking down at her.

She kept absolutely still, but the increased tenor of her breathing must have given her away, because he said softly: 'Move over!'

Helen gasped. 'Your—your bed is over there,' she stammered.

'This is my bed,' remarked Jake huskily, and without waiting for her permission he slid beneath the covers, his warm body close against hers. Helen panicked, and she tried to get out of the bed at the other side, but his arm prevented her.

'Don't fight me, Helen,' he groaned urgently, his mouth seeking the soft curve of her neck. 'Don't you know you've nearly driven me out of my mind this evening? Dear God—I *want you*!'

Helen tried desperately to resist him, but it was no use. He was stronger than she was, and besides, the age-old desire of Eve to taste the forbidden fruit of the apple was upon her.

Once before morning he woke her again, his mouth warm and insistent, and this time she did not resist him, but responded as eagerly as he, without caring of the consequences. This was her man, her husband, and she loved him with every fibre of her being.

But when morning did come, and the room was flooded with the pale gold of sunlight, Jake was gone. Only the fact that his bed had not been slept in bore witness to the fact that he had spent the night in hers. . .

CHAPTER EIGHT

HELEN rolled over lazily and looked at her watch. She was amazed to discover it was already half past ten and she slid immediately out of bed, shivering, as the cold air hit her warm body. Reaching for her dressing gown, she made her way to the bathroom and felt much more refreshed after a brisk shower. Then she dressed in navy trousers and a ribbed jumper with short sleeves and leaving her hair loose went downstairs.

Only Mujari was in the living room, stoking up the already roaring fire, and he smiled a greeting at her. Helen hesitated a moment and then said: 'Where is everybody, Mujari?'

Mujari frowned. 'Missus Rose, she is in the kitchen. Mr Lucien and Mr Jake, they out.' He smiled again. 'You want I tell Missus Rose?'

'That won't be necessary, Mujari, I'm here.' Rose came slowly into the room. 'I heard voices, so I guessed you were up at last, Helen. You have slept well. Jake said not to disturb you.'

Hot colour stained Helen's cheeks, but Rose merely wagged her finger at her mischievously. 'Now, don't go making any excuses to me,' she

said. 'I understand perfectly, believe me.' She
smiled reminiscently. 'Jake is such an attractive
man, I could fall for him myself.'

Helen didn't know what to reply to that, but
she said, as casually as she could: 'Er—where
are Lucien and Jake?'

Rose spread her hands. 'They have gone for a
walk. To look at the village, they said. Myself, I
think they are talking business again. Lucien is
most eager to have this complex of Jake's in
Tsaba. It will provide a lot of jobs for a lot of
people, and bring money as well as prestige to
the country.'

Helen nodded. 'I see. And did Lucien tell you
when they expect to leave?'

Rose shrugged. 'Within the next few days, I
should think. Why? Don't you want Jake to go
away again so soon?'

Helen shook her head helplessly. Until now
she had not dared to consider what she wanted.
She didn't even know what was to happen. How
could she explain her anxieties to Rose, who
naturally assumed theirs was a normal marriage?
She knew Jake's reputation with women who
demanded anything of him. And he had never
said he loved her. He had said he *wanted* her, but
that was a vastly different proposition.

For a moment she allowed herself to recall the
last few hours spent in Jake's arms. For her it
had been a miraculous insight into what love

between a man and a woman could be. She had not dreamt such heights of ecstasy could be scaled, or that Jake could be so patient, teaching her to abandon herself in a way that caused the hot colour to flood her cheeks at its remembrance. Rose watched her curiously, and then she said: 'It's obvious you don't want him to go. Why don't you go with him?'

Helen stared at her incredulously. 'What did you say?'

'I said go with them. Why not? You don't have to stay in England, do you? You've no commitments, have you?'

'No, but—' Helen tucked a strand of hair behind her ear. 'I—I don't know.'

Rose shrugged again. 'I would be in no doubt if it were me. Without this—' she patted her stomach '—without this, I would go like a shot from a gun!'

'Would you?' Helen sounded wistful. 'Oh, but it's your country—your home.'

Rose raised her eyebrows. 'Yes. But I came here with Lucien. I didn't have to. We could have stayed in Luanya, that's the capital, where we live. I could have stayed there and Lucien would have visited me regularly.'

'But you're the Ambassador's wife! You have to accompany him.'

Rose sighed. 'Maybe so. Maybe not. But I would not let Lucien out of my sight.'

Helen smiled. Rose's ideas were very simple, but she had no idea of the complications that had arisen in Helen's previously ordered life.

The men came back at lunchtime while Helen was alone in the living room, Rose having disappeared to supervise the serving of the meal. Lucien came in first, rubbing his hands to warm them.

'Hello, sleepyhead!' he remarked cheerfully. 'What time did you wake up?'

'About ten-thirty,' replied Helen ruefully, half dreading the moment when Jake must come through the door.

'Ten-thirty!' Lucien looked suitably scandalised, and was making some laughing comment about early to bed, early to rise, when Jake came into the room.

This morning he was wearing the dark suede trousers he had worn to travel down, and a mauve silk shirt. A charcoal grey suede waistcoat hung loosely from his shoulders, and he looked big and muscular and ominously sombre.

Helen looked up at him nervously, but she was unable to read his expression. He was much too adept at hiding his feelings, and a cold chill of apprehension filled the pit of her stomach. How stupid she had been to imagine that what they had shared meant anything special to him. She kept her eyes focused intently on her hands in her lap, and even when Lucien offered her a sherry she scarcely looked up, taking the glass gratefully, holding it between her fingers.

Lucien disappeared to see his wife, and Helen's nerves stretched. What now? What derisive comment was to be forthcoming?

But Jake did not immediately say anything, swallowing his beer and helping himself to a second. Then he came to stand on the hearth before the fire, looking down on her penetratingly, making an impatient exclamation when she said nothing and did not even look up.

'Helen!' he muttered grimly. 'I have to talk to you.'

'Not now,' she said, swallowing a little of her sherry. 'I—er—where have you been this morning?'

'*Helen!*' His voice was tormented. 'Look at me!'

But just at that moment Lisa Harding came into the room, smiling warmly at Jake.

'Jake!' she exclaimed. 'So you're back. Mrs Ndana said you'd gone for a walk with her husband. I seem to have seen so little of you this weekend.'

Jake made a deprecative movement of his shoulders. 'It's been a short visit,' he said casually. 'After all, we didn't arrive until nearly lunchtime yesterday and we're leaving immediately after lunch today.'

'Oh, Jake!' Lisa pouted charmingly. 'Still, you

will come to see us in London again, won't you? It seems ages since we talked over old times.'

Helen rose abruptly to her feet. 'Excuse me,' she said, feeling slightly sick, and despite Jake's attempt to catch her wrist she evaded him and made her way to their bedroom, flinging herself on the bed with careless disregard for the clothes. In that moment she felt she wanted to die. . .

The sound of Rose calling her name forced her back to reality. She was telling her that lunch was ready, and Helen knew she would have to go down and try and behave naturally.

The meal seemed endless, and after it was over she was immensely glad to see Mujari putting their cases in the boot of the Ferrari.

'Well, Jake,' Lucien said warmly, 'it's been good to see you. I'll give you a ring on Monday when I get back to town, and we'll arrange the final details, eh?'

'Fine, Lucien. G'bye, Rose.'

'Goodbye, Jake. Goodbye, Helen. Drive carefully!'

The Ferrari moved away smoothly, and Helen waved until they were out of sight. Then she lay back in her seat and rested a protective wrist across her forehead. The effort of behaving naturally had placed an immense strain upon her, and now she felt drained.

Jake drove for several miles in silence, and then when they emerged on to the main road, he said: 'So now we talk, right?'

Helen shook her head bewilderedly. 'What is there to talk about?' she asked, in a frozen voice.

Jake uttered a muffled curse. 'Stop being obtuse, Helen. You know damn nicely what we have to talk about.' He swung expertly round a curve in the road. 'Last night!'

Helen heaved a sigh. 'I—I'd rather not talk about that, if you don't mind—'

'Well, I do mind!' he ground out savagely. 'For God's sake, Helen, at least give me the chance to apologise.'

'Apologise?' Helen stared at his profile confusedly.

'Yes, damn you, apologise! God, I don't know what came over me! And then when I found you were—well—untouched, I still couldn't leave you alone.' His fingers tightened grimly on the steering wheel. 'I don't know if you believe this, but it will never happen again!'

Helen caught her breath. 'Jake, please! Stop making a federal case out of it! I—I'm not a child, after all. I—I knew what I was doing.'

'Did you? Did you really?' Jake chewed violently at his lower lip. 'Don't bother to try and appease me! I know I'm a swine! But believe me, I'm not proud of it!'

Helen twisted her palms in her lap. 'Please! This is ridiculous! There's no need for this postmortem—'

Jake glanced swiftly at her pale face. 'Why don't you swear at me or something? I deserve it. Why do you take it all so blasted indifferently?'

Helen looked quickly away from him. He thought she was indifferent! Oh, God, she thought achingly. If only she was!

After that, there was silence for a long while, and once they got on to the motorway Jake put his foot down and they were soon approaching the outskirts of the city.

Mrs Latimer greeted them when they arrived at Kersland Square and asked them if they had had dinner.

Jake shook his head. 'No, we haven't,' he replied.

'But don't bother doing anything for me. I'm—I'm going out.'

Helen's face tightened. He was going out. *Where?*

She wanted to say: *'Don't go! Stay with me! Make love to me!'*

But of course she could not and instead she said quietly: 'Don't do anything for me either, Mrs Latimer. I—I think I'll have an early night. Just—a cup of coffee and a sandwich will do.'

Mrs Latimer departed to get Helen's supper and Jake stood hesitatingly in the hall. He had carried their cases upstairs and was now looking thoughtfully at Helen, his eyes dark and intent.

'You do look tired,' he said quietly. 'I'm sorry.'

'Oh, stop it!' Helen's voice rose shrilly as she spoke. She couldn't bear solicitude from him. 'For heaven's sake, go and leave me alone!'

Jake stared at her impotently. 'Helen, don't let this—spoil things—'

'Spoil things! *Spoil things!*' Helen infused a deliberately scathing note into her voice. 'What is there to spoil? Heavens, Jake, what century do you think this is? Put what happened down to circumstances—to the particularly good wine we'd been drinking. It was good wine, wasn't it?'

'Helen!' Jake's voice was stern now. 'Stop this.'

'Stop what? Talking sensibly about something that happens every day in much less salubrious circumstances? You're old-fashioned, Jake. I wouldn't have believed it, but you are!'

'Helen!' Jake caught her by the shoulders and shook her hard. 'Stop it! Don't think you can fool me by behaving like this! I know what I've done better than anyone. All I want to do right now is soak myself in Scotch until I can't even think—let alone feel!'

Helen twisted away from him. 'Then go on. I don't care.'

Jake stood his ground. 'What will you do?'

'Me?' Helen was having immense difficulty in holding back the tears that trembled behind her eyes. 'I told Mrs Latimer, I'm going to have an early night.'

Jake hunched his shoulders. 'And can I trust you to do just that?'

'Why not?' Helen put a hand on the banister rail. 'There doesn't seem much else to do, does there?'

Jake raked a hand through his hair and suddenly she thought he looked rather young and vulnerable somehow. But that was ridiculous, she told herself fiercely; there was nothing vulnerable about Jake Howard!'

'Well, if you're sure you'll be okay—'

'Of course I'm sure!' Helen held her head up determinedly. 'Oh—oh, by the way, when do you leave for Tsaba?'

Jake hunched his shoulders. 'On Wednesday, probably—why? Don't you want me to go?' His eyes darkened.

Helen spread a careless hand. 'It's of complete indifference to me what you do!' she remarked, with deliberate contempt, and as though that was sufficient for him, Jake turned and strode out of the door, slamming it behind him.

Helen was dreaming, and it was a horrible dream. She was out in the driving rain, running up the muddy track towards the Morgans' farm, but when she got near she could see that it wasn't the Morgans' farm at all but the house in Kersland Square, curiously detached from its fellow dwellings. She stopped, put a hand to her head and stared. Jennifer's car was outside, and a terrible feeling of foreboding gripped her. She ran up the steps and into the hall and then she could hear laughter, lots and lots of feminine laughter coming from upstairs. She climbed the stairs slowly, afraid of what she was about to find but driven on by some terrible urge to know the truth. She thrust open the door of Jake's bedroom, and he was there—with a woman—but when the woman turned Helen could see it wasn't Jennifer at all but Lisa Harding.

'*No!*' Helen was conscious of herself saying the word over and over again, wildly, disbelievingly, tormentedly, and Lisa caught her cruelly by the shoulders and began shaking her and shaking her. . .

'Helen! Helen! Calm down! You're all right. You're safe—here—at home.'

Helen opened her eyes with difficulty, the pale lamplight illuminating the face of the man above her who was gently shaking her awake. She was breathing gulpingly, chokingly, as though she had been doing something strenuous, her face wet with tears.

She blinked rapidly, her breathing slowing as she recognised Jake's anxious features. 'What— what is it? What's wrong?' she whispered.

Jake allowed her to rest against the soft pillows. 'You've been dreaming,' he said, sitting down on the side of the bed, smoothing damp tendrils of her hair back behind her ears. 'You've been very distressed. I thought for a minute a burglar was in the house.' He smiled, his eyes more gentle than she had ever seen them.

'I'm—I'm sorry!' Helen put a hand to her head. 'I—I've never done that before.'

Jake's eyes darkened. 'I know. I guess it was a hangover from this blasted weekend.' He shook his head impatiently. 'Are you all right now?'

Helen heaved a sigh. 'Yes, I think so,' she said, her eyes feeding on him, loving him, watching every small movement he made. His hair was tousled from his bed and he was dressed in a navy silk dressing gown, and from his appearance she didn't somehow think he had spent the night drinking as he had said he was going to do.

Jake rose to his feet. 'I'll go, then. Goodnight, Helen.'

'Wait!' Helen propped herself up on one elbow and caught his fingers. 'Jake—don't go!'

Jake's colour deepened. 'I thought you said you were all right now—' and then at the look in her green eyes he uttered an expletive. 'For God's sake, Helen, you don't know what you're asking!'

'I do.' Helen raised his hand to her lips, but Jake snatched it abruptly away, striding swiftly to the door. He didn't look back and the door banged hollowly behind him, as hollow as the feeling Helen was experiencing at his rejection. . .

Selby railway station was not the most inspiring of places on a damp cold November afternoon, and Helen was glad of the warmth of her sheepskin coat over the thick trouser suit she was wearing. She carried only one small suitcase and after she had handed in her ticket she went outside to hire a cab. She had Mrs Howard's address from occasional communications, Christmas cards and things, and she gave this to the driver, settling into the corner of the cab to wait apprehensively for their arrival.

She didn't really know what had put the idea of coming to Jake's mother into her head, unless perhaps it had been Jennifer's attitude.

She had awakened this morning with an awful sense of foreboding hanging over her head, and with coherency had come the painful remembrance of what she had done. Even now, a wave of humiliation swept over her as she recalled Jake's instant rejection of her, and she had been overwhelmingly relieved to discover he had already left the house before she got up.

During a lonely breakfast of coffee and cigarettes she had tried to assimilate her position and had come to the only conclusion possible. She could no longer go on living with Jake, knowing he despised her, afraid of her own weakness creating further humiliation. She would ask him for a divorce and somehow it would be arranged. These things were not difficult to contrive these days, and she didn't much care who was cited as the guilty party.

But then had come the realisation that she could not stay here, in Jake's house. She would have to find somewhere else to stay. But where? And with whom? The idea of a lonely bedsitter was chilling but eventually to be a fact. After all, she could not expect maintenance from Jake. She was a perfectly healthy individual, and there was no possible reason why she should not get a job.

She thought about his proposed trip to Africa. If she could just keep out of his way until then by the time he came back she would have herself under control again. Just now she felt she was emotionally unstable, unable to cope with any more arguments.

So she rang Jennifer and told her what she intended to do. Jennifer was obviously shocked, but as she had no idea of the real facts of the situation she was not much help.

'But, darling,' she exclaimed, 'you've known what Jake is like for years! Why the sudden decision to break up your marriage? Heavens, I always thought you didn't give a damn what he did.'

Helen swallowed hard. 'Perhaps I'm getting sick and tired of such an artificial relationship,'

she said carefully. 'Maybe I want a real
marriage—a family.'

'Oh, God, Helen! You can't be serious!'

'Why not?'

'Why not? Well, because, darling, you're not
the type. I can't see you appreciating the less
attractive necessities of motherhood. And just
think of being pregnant! I ask you—who wants
to go around for nine months getting steadily
uglier and uglier!'

Helen's fingers had clenched round the phone.
She had wanted to shout: *'Me! I do! Just so long
as it was Jake's baby I was bearing!'*

But instead she said nothing of the kind, and
allowed Jennifer to attempt to persuade her to be
sensible. And then she had rung off and sat for
a long while just staring at the phone.

And that was when the idea had occurred to
her. If she went to Selby, to Jake's mother's, he
would not know where she was. And certainly
he would never think of looking for her there. He
would go off to Tsaba, and once he had left the
country she would return to London, pack her
things, and put the matter in the hands of a
solicitor.

The rain-wet windows of the cab mirrored the
drab scene outside. Mothers and children hurried
home from the shops, workmen stood in queues
for buses, cars splashed through puddles, drench-
ing anyone near enough to be soaked by the

muddy spray that ensued. This was Jake's home town, the place he had been born, where he had gone to school and learned that he had a brain.

Helen sighed. It was a shocking thing that in all the years of their marriage she had never been here before.

She thought of what reception she might receive from his mother. She had what she had to say all planned. After all, Mrs Howard had never wanted her to marry her son, so by rights she should be glad that Helen was here. But would she appreciate Helen's anxieties that Jake might have tried to find her in London and persuade her to return to him? Would she understand that right now Helen was in no fit state to resist such a request? And would she help her to keep out of sight until Jake was safely in Tsaba, thus giving her nearly two months to make another life for herself?

Mrs Latimer had looked at her strangely this morning when she had gone out with her suitcase. She had made some excuse about taking some old books to the hospital, but she was sure Mrs Latimer didn't believe her. Still, there was nothing she could do now and she had made sure no one had heard her give the name of King's Cross station to the cab driver.

Now she returned her thoughts to the present and saw that they had left the main thoroughfare and were traversing some narrow side streets.

Rows of terraced houses closed in about her and she sat forward in her seat studying the names of the streets intently.

At last she saw the name she was looking for: Harrison Terrace, and there was number thirty-seven.

The cab driver drew in to the kerb and Helen climbed out, looking up at the narrow house where Jake had been born. Then she hastily fumbled in her bag for a five pound note and shook her head when the driver began searching his pockets for change.

He touched his cap politely and stood her suit-case on the step, then he got back into his cab and drove away.

Helen knocked at the door. The lace-curtained windows revealed nothing of what was inside and she felt her heart hammering uncomfortably. Presently, however, the door was opened by an elderly woman, and Helen staring at her anxiously recognised Mrs Howard's firm features.

'Yes?' she began politely, and then she gasped, pressing a hand to her mouth. 'Good lord, it's— Helen—isn't it? What's wrong? Has there been an accident? Is Jake ill?'

Helen shook her head vigorously. 'No, no, nothing like that. Jake doesn't even know I'm here. He—he's fine.'

Mrs Howard frowned in a puzzled way and

then she stepped back abruptly. 'I suppose you'd better come in, then.'

'Thank you.' Helen stepped past her mother-in-law into the narrow hall that ran from front to back of the house.

Mrs Howard closed the door and then opened a door a little further down the hall. 'We can go in here.'

The room they entered was the lace-curtained one overlooking the street. It was cold and cheerless without a fire, very clean and neat, obviously seldom used.

'Oh, please,' exclaimed Helen awkwardly. 'I'm sure this isn't where you were sitting. Couldn't we go there?'

Mrs Howard hesitated. 'Will what you have to say take long?'

Helen sighed. 'I'm afraid it might.'

Jake's mother bit her lip. 'Oh, well,' she said grudgingly. 'All right, we'll go through into the kitchen. It's certainly warmer there.'

The kitchen was as large as the other room, with a comfortable fireplace and armchairs, and an alcove leading off which housed the sink and gas cooker. Mrs Howard waved Helen to take one of the armchairs and then she seemed to notice the suitcase in Helen's hand, for she frowned again, and said: 'I'll just put the kettle on.'

Helen smiled and sank into an armchair, loosening her coat. All of a sudden she felt exhausted, and this cheerful little room seemed the most welcome place on earth. She felt secure here, and safe, too. Safe from making a fool of herself over this woman's son.

Mrs Howard came back and stood before her, rubbing her hands together doubtfully. 'Now then, lass,' she said, 'what's wrong?'

Helen sighed. 'Won't you sit down too?'

Mrs Howard shrugged. 'All right. There—now tell me.'

Helen sought about for a suitable way to begin. 'First of all, I should tell you, Jake and I are going to divorce.'

'What?' Mrs Howard was flabbergasted. 'But he's never said the like to me.'

Helen bent her head. 'No—well, it's all been decided rather suddenly. In actual fact, Jake hasn't really agreed.'

'Come now, lass, how can you be getting a divorce if our Jake hasn't agreed?'

Helen shook her head. 'Well, I want a divorce, Mrs Howard. And that's final. Oh, you know you didn't want me to marry him in the first place. Well, you were right. We're not suited.'

'I see.' Mrs Howard got up to make tea in a china teapot. 'But why are you here?'

Helen wetted her dry lips. 'Last night—last night we had—a row. I—I've walked out. I wanted to get out of London until he leaves for

Tsaba, and I knew he'd never think of looking for me here.'

'Tsaba?' Mrs Howard came back with the tray of tea. 'What's that?'

'It's a country—in Central Africa. Jake knows their ambassador.'

Mrs Howard frowned. 'Oh, yes, I remember now. Isn't their name Ndana or something? They're the couple Jake got Lisa Harding a job with.'

Helen felt a pain in her stomach like a knife. 'That's right,' she managed chokingly. 'Well— well, Jake's going out there, on Wednesday, I think. If—if I could just stay here until he's left town—'

'Stay here?' Mrs Howard sounded astounded. 'But why here? Surely you've friends of your own who would keep you? I've never heard the like! Coming here, asking me to take your side against my son!'

'No! No, it's not like that.' Helen thrust her tea aside impatiently. 'Don't you see, I thought you'd be pleased.'

'Why? Because Jake's marriage is splitting up?'

'His marriage to *me*! Yes.'

Mrs Howard compressed her lips. 'I thought Jake was happy. He always seemed contented enough when he came here.'

Helen rose abruptly to her feet. 'So you won't help me, then.'

Mrs Howard rose too. 'Now hold on, hold on, lass,' she said steadily. 'I never said any such thing. But you can't expect to come here and explode a bombshell like that and not have any reaction. Good lord, we're not your fashionable London set. In Selby marriage means something more than lines on a bit of paper!'

'It means more than that to me, too,' protested Helen quickly. 'That's why I want a divorce.'

Mrs Howard shook her head. 'But I don't understand. I was always under the impression you married Jake—well, because he could provide you with a meal ticket for life! What's happened now? Has some other chap come along with a better proposition?'

Helen's cheeks paled at that and Mrs Howard looked a little shamefaced. 'All right, all right,' she said, 'I'll take that back. But you must admit you weren't in love with Jake when you married him.'

'I know.' Helen sank down into her chair again. 'And I suppose I did marry him for the reasons you said, except that I chose him for a very special reason. I knew it would horrify my father's family.' She looked up. 'They cut him off, you see, because he wasn't like them. They're very much of the old school of aristocracy, county and all that! Jake was the very antithesis of everything my uncle stands for, and I married him partly because of that.'

'I see.' Mrs Howard sat down again too and heaved a sigh. 'But now you want to be free?'

Helen swallowed hard. 'You could put it like that.'

'Then why couldn't you have waited until he'd gone to Tsaba? Surely a couple of days wouldn't make much difference after three years and more?'

'*No!*' Helen was adamant. 'I—I had to get away. I'm sorry, but there it is.' Her voice broke ignominiously, and Mrs Howard stood up again, taking away the tea tray and generally avoiding Helen's obvious distress.

By the time she came back Helen had herself under control again, and Mrs Howard stood looking at her consideringly. 'You can stay,' she said abruptly. 'You can have Jake's room. He won't be needing it.'

Helen rose now. 'Oh, thank you! Thank you.'

Mrs Howard shook her head deprecatingly. 'Don't thank me. I don't even know if I'm doing the right thing. But you're obviously too upset right now to argue about it. Come along, I'll show you the room and then I'll see about something to eat.'

Helen nodded silently. There was something strong and reassuring about Mrs Howard. Like Jake, she had no time for pretence.

CHAPTER NINE

Miss Frazer burst into tears, and Jake rested his chin on his fist, supporting himself with his elbow on his desk. He regarded the girl resignedly, and then sighed with ill-concealed impatience.

'All right, Miss Frazer, all right,' he said heavily. 'I'm sorry. We'll go over that again. Now, did you get as far as the chemical analysis? You did? Good. Then we can start from there.' He consulted the papers on his desk and began dictating once again, and the young woman opposite him scribbled frantically in her shorthand notebook.

Jake's secretary, Linda Holland, was absent from work this morning and he was using his general manager's secretary as her replacement, but while Sheila Frazer was an adequate secretary she was not in Linda's class, and Jake, impatient to finish his work and leave the office, was in no mood to be tolerant. Already he had had to repeat himself several times, spelling out the chemical substances referred to with increasing repetition, and a few moments ago he had lost his temper and snapped angrily at her.

At last the dictation was over and Jake thrust

the papers irritably aside. 'You can get Mr Mainwaring to sign them,' he said broodingly. 'You will be able to read your shorthand, won't you?'

'I—I think so, Mr Howard.' Miss Frazer rose unhappily to her feet. 'Is that all, sir?'

Jake chewed moodily at his lips and looked up absently as she spoke. 'What? Oh—oh, yes, yes, that's all. I'm sorry if I upset you.' His eyes were cool, detached.

Sheila Frazer smiled appealingly. 'That's all right, Mr Howard. Thank you.'

Jake nodded, watching her disappear through the door which led to his secretary's office, and then pushing back his chair abruptly he got to his feet.

He walked to the window of the huge office, looking out on a vista of the city. His apartments were the penthouse of the building and he had a magnificent view from here. Turning, he surveyed his office without pleasure. Large and well lit, softly carpeted in dark blue, with dark mahogany furniture, it was the epitome of what a business room should be, and he had always felt a certain pride of possession, knowing himself the power behind the throne.

But today there was no pleasure in anything. He felt physically sick, and an ache in the region of his temples had nothing to do with the shortage of sleep he had had the night before. In all his life there had never been anything he had wanted which had seemed inevitably out of his grasp. Power, position, success, money; they had all been goals he had reached for and attained, but the thing he wanted now was unattainable.

He uttered a grim curse, and flung himself bitterly back into his chair. He closed his eyes for a moment, endeavouring to shut out the images that came to plague his mind, but it was useless. Jake Howard, the man who had always prided himself on being able to handle anything and anybody, had made a complete hash-up of his own marriage.

He leant forward, resting his arms on the desk, trying to understand why he had never realised what was happening to him until it was too late. When he had arrived back from the States and found Helen out with Keith Mannering he had been furious, but he had thought that that was all it was: anger! He had never dreamt it might have its basis in that tortuous agony called jealousy. But as the weeks went by it had become more and more obvious that his whole life was being shaken by that primitive force. Of course he had not accepted it, even then. Why would he? He had imagined Helen to be an ice-maiden, cool and aloof, indifferent to the sexual side of marriage.

But gradually his own emotions had become involved, almost against his will, and he had found himself watching her, wanting her, needing her, until he could no longer act sanely. But that didn't excuse his behaviour. Nothing could do that.

This weekend everything had exploded, and he had found himself in a situation from which there seemed no escape. His actions had destroyed the slender thread of any relationship they might have sustained. Recalling the reproach in her eyes yesterday morning, he despised himself anew.

He buried his face in his hands as he remembered her fear the night before. What terrible nightmare had caused her to scream in her sleep? What manner of monster did she think he was? And when, in her terror, she had begged him to stay he had been unable to do it. He had known full well that he could no longer trust himself where she was concerned.

With a grim tightening of his jaw he rose abruptly to his feet. He could not stay here any longer. He wanted to go home, to see Helen, to try and explain what it was that had driven him to put such a wedge between them. Could he make her see that her involvement with Mannering was eating him up? That no matter what had gone before, he had fallen in love with her, could not visualise life without her?

He thought of the women he had known and his lips twisted. Since his return from the United States he had not even looked at another woman, let alone slept with one. He, Jake Howard, was trapped in the very mesh he had sworn never to tangle with.

He went down in the lift, responding automatically to the polite greetings of his employees. The commissionaire opened his car door for him and touched his cap respectfully. Everything was exactly the same as it had always been, but it no longer gave him any pleasure.

He drove home to the house in Kersland Square, and entered the attractive hall, noticing that Mrs Latimer had put new flowers in the vase on the chest. Mrs Latimer herself appeared as he entered, and smiled politely at him.

'Good afternoon, sir,' she said, and Jake glanced swiftly at his watch, scarcely realising it was after twelve.

'Good afternoon, Mrs Latimer.' Jake was impatient. 'Where's my wife?'

Mrs Latimer folded the coat he had thrown off carelessly. 'Mrs Howard isn't at home, sir. She went out about ten o'clock.'

'*Damn!*' Jake heaved an irritated sigh. 'Did she say where she was going? When she'd be back?'

'She had a suitcase with her, sir. She said she was taking some old books to the hospital—'

Jake interrupted her, his eyes diamond hard. 'What books? What hospital?'

'I don't know, sir. Like I said, she was on her way out when she told me.'

'*God almighty!*' Jake ran a hand round the back

of his neck, tautening the silk shirt across his broad chest. A terrible feeling of anxiety was growing inside him, and he felt physically ill.

'Shall I get your lunch now, sir—'

'Lunch! *Lunch!*' Jake grunted. 'I don't want anything to eat. Oh, go on, then, a sandwich, that's all!' This at the look of hurt expectation on Mrs Latimer's face.

'Yes, sir.' Worriedly she hung his coat in the hall closet and then disappeared through the door into her own domain. Jake stood where he had left her and then on impulse he lifted the phone.

Looking in the book beside the instrument, he found Jennifer's number and dialled it impatiently. A maid answered and a few moments later Jennifer's light tones came over the wire. 'Jake darling, how marvellous! Have you rung to invite me out for lunch, because I'm free!'

Jake waited until she had finished laughing, and then said: 'I want to know if you know where Helen is.'

Jennifer was taken aback. 'Helen? Helen? Isn't she with you?'

'If she were, would I be ringing you?' Jake was terse.

'No, of course not. Sorry, darling. And no— no, I don't know where she is. Have you lost her?'

Jake kept his temper with difficulty. 'You might say that.'

'Oh, *dear!*' Jennifer sounded insinuative.

'What is that supposed to mean?'

'What, darling?' Jennifer pretended ignorance.

'That certain way you said "oh, dear". What was the implication behind it?'

'Oh, nothing.' Jennifer seemed to be considering. 'Just—just things!'

'What things?' Jake was beginning to feel that if he had Jennifer within reaching distance he would strangle her.

'Just something Helen said this morning on the phone, darling.'

'Helen rang you? This morning?'

'Yes, darling. Didn't she tell you?'

'I wasn't here,' replied Jake grimly. 'Well? What did she say?'

'I don't really know whether I ought to tell you, darling. I mean—it might have been in confidence, after all.'

'Jennifer, I warn you—'

Jennifer giggled softly. 'Oh, darling, I love that masterful note in your voice!' Then she sobered with a sigh. 'Actually, she said she was thinking of leaving you.'

'Of what?' Jake was incredulous.

'Of leaving you, darling. Yes, I was surprised, too.'

Jake could feel anger rising inside him. 'Did she say why?'

Jennifer sounded doubtful. 'Not really, darling. I think she was just feeling down in the dumps.

Your weekend in Wales doesn't appear to have done her much good. Whatever happened? Was it all terribly boring?'

Jake clenched his fists. 'Perhaps,' he said, noncommittally. 'So you've no idea where she is, then?'

'None whatsoever, darling. Unless—unless—'

'Unless what?' Jake was abrupt.

'Well, unless she's at Keith's home!'

'Mannering?' Jake felt the ball of his anger like an actual physical thing inside him.

'Well, I'm only suggesting, darling. She is—fond of him, isn't she?'

'Is she? I'm not aware of that.' Jake was cold.

Jennifer sounded doubtful now. 'Jake, don't take my word for it. I mean—well, she could be at the hairdresser's, couldn't she?'

Jake saw Mrs Latimer returning with his sandwiches and heaved a sigh. 'Yes, yes, I guess she could be at that.'

'Do let me know when you find her, won't you?' Jennifer tried to hold his attention. 'Jake—Jake, are you still there?'

'Yes, yes, all right, Jennifer. G'bye.'

He rang off before he was tempted to say more than he should and looked thoughtfully at Mrs Latimer. The housekeeper carried the tray into the lounge and put it down on the low table before the fireplace, straightening as Jake came into the room. Jake saw the anxious expression in her face and said:

'You're absolutely certain Mrs Howard didn't say where she was going?'

'No, sir.' Mrs Latimer shook her head. 'But I shouldn't worry, sir. She's often out for lunch.'

Jake's brows drew together. 'Is she? With whom?'

'Mrs St John mostly. Occasionally with—with Mr Mannering.'

'Oh, yes, Mannering!' Jake's expression grew cynical. 'Tell me, what do you think Mrs Howard's relationship with Mr Mannering is?'

'Oh, sir—' Mrs Latimer looked shocked.

Jake raised his dark eyebrows. 'Well?'

'It's not my place to wonder about things like that, sir.'

'No, but you must have your own ideas.' Jake was ruthlessly determined to find out, regardless of the ethics involved. 'Well?'

'She scarcely knows him, sir.'

'While I was away—in the States—was she ever away overnight?'

'Only in Wiltshire, sir. With Mr and Mrs St John. She left me their telephone number in case you called.'

'I see.' Jake flung himself into an armchair, his head throbbing quite painfully by now. 'So in your opinion my wife couldn't be there?'

'Where, sir?'

'With Mannering?'

Mrs Latimer looked horrified. 'With Mr Mannering, sir? Heavens, why should you think she might be there?'

Jake shook his head. 'I don't know,' he muttered, running a hand over his eyes. 'God, I'm tired!'

'Then why don't you rest this afternoon, sir? I can tell Mrs Howard when she gets back—'

She was interrupted by the sound of the telephone, and Jake was out of his chair and out of the door before she had time to forestall him.

'Yes?' he said curtly. 'Howard speaking.'

'Jake! Is that you? Lucien here.'

Jake's shoulders sagged. 'Oh, God, Lucien, yes. Yes? What can I do for you?'

'Is something wrong, man?' Lucien sounded perturbed.

'No—no, nothing.'

'Well, if you say so. I rang to let you know my secretary has arranged the flight tickets and so on. We leave at seven a.m. Wednesday morning—'

'Look, Lucien!' Jake heaved a sigh. 'Look, I don't know if I'm going to be able to make that deadline.'

'What? Why? You're not backing out on me, are you, Jake?'

'God, no!' Jake raked a hand through his hair.

'Look, how would it be if I got Martindale to accompany you?'

'But I thought you were keen to see the site for yourself.' Lucien sounded hurt now.

'I was. I *am*. But something's come up.'

'More important than the deal? It must be big, man.'

'It is.' Jake sighed again. 'Okay, Lucien, Helen's disappeared.'

'What?'

'I said Helen's disappeared—'

'I heard you, Jake.' Lucien uttered an exclamation. 'But why? What's wrong?'

'I can't explain right now.' Jake glanced round to see whether Mrs Latimer was listening but she had disappeared into her kitchen when he answered the phone. 'Look, I'll get in touch with Martindale and arrange something with him.'

'You can't brief him in a couple of days!' exclaimed Lucien. 'No, leave it, Jake, and I'll call off the trip for the present. It can wait a couple of weeks, sure it can. But let us know about Helen, won't you? I wish there was something I could do.'

'There's nothing. But thanks anyway, Lucien. I appreciate it.'

'Think nothing of it, man.'

Jake made some suitable rejoinder and then rang off, staring for a while at the phone before turning and going back into the lounge. But the sight of the sandwiches revolted him and he poured himself a stiff whisky before mounting the stairs to his room.

He loosened his tie as he went through the door. Perhaps a shower would clear his brain. Right now, he felt positively fuddled. And that was when he saw the letter. It was standing against the pillows on his bed, stark and white against the apricot counterpane.

Jake swallowed the remainder of his scotch at a gulp, and snatched up the letter, ripping open the envelope carelessly. The note inside was depressingly brief and to the point. It said simply:

I can't go on after what happened. Don't try to find me. I'll be in touch when I find somewhere to live. Helen.

Jake read the note twice and then tore it up into tiny pieces, staring grimly out of the window as he did so. *I can't go on after what happened!* Her words repeated themselves over and over in his head. He might have known that a woman of Helen's nervous temperament could not accept any apology he might make. To her he was simply a predator, taking what he wanted with complete disregard for the consequences, and she would never trust him again.

He flung off his tie and dropped it disinterestedly on the floor. His jacket and shirt followed it, and finally his trousers, pants, shoes and socks. Then he walked into the bathroom and turned on the shower, allowing the refreshing stream of water to soak his hair as well as his body.

When he finally emerged, his brain felt alert again, and he was able to think more coherently. But in spite of that the headache persisted, and with it his concern to know Helen's whereabouts.

He dressed in a blue lounge suit and went downstairs again. He had decided to go and see Keith Mannering. Regardless of whether Helen was involved with him or otherwise, he had to know what she had told him about their marriage.

Keith was at his office and clearly disturbed when Jake was shown into his presence by a smiling secretary.

'I don't have a lot of time,' he began awkwardly. 'My father is expecting me at—'

'What I have to say won't take much time,' retorted Jake, interrupting him. 'Have you seen Helen since we got back from Wales?'

'Wales? I didn't even know you were going to Wales.'

'Okay, okay, I'll accept that.' Jake put a cheroot between his teeth. 'So tell me, exactly what is your interest in my wife?'

Keith's cheeks reddened. 'I thought you knew—at least—we're friends, that's all. Good friends!'

'I see.' Jake lit his cheroot and drew on it deeply. 'You wouldn't have any plans beyond that?'

'She's married to you, Mr Howard!' Keith was stiff.

'Yes, I know.' Jake exhaled smoke into the air above their heads, his manner cool and detached.

And then with an abrupt *volte-face* he reached out a hand and caught Keith's shirt front in a savage grip, dragging the other man closer to him.

'I say—' Keith protested hotly. 'You can't come in here—'

'I can do exactly what I like!' bit out Jake in a distinct voice. 'And if I find you've laid a hand on my wife, I'll take you apart myself. Do I make myself clear?'

He released Keith just as abruptly as he had taken hold of him and the younger man staggered a little before gaining his balance. 'I—I could have you up for assault!' he exclaimed indignantly.

'Try it!' Jake said pleasantly, and turning on his heel he walked out of the office.

For the rest of the day he was involved with work. He had had to go back to the office and once there a dozen queries awaited his attention. He dealt with them all with the detachment he had shown in Keith Mannering's office, but inside he was obsessed with learning Helen's whereabouts. At times he came close to hating her for walking out on him like this without even bothering to leave an address, and he mentally went through all her friends, trying to think of someone to whom she might turn.

But apart from Jennifer there was no one of consequence. Helen was not the type to pour her troubles out to all and sundry, and somehow he couldn't see her approaching any of the sophisticated set they moved in.

The worst time of day came after dinner, after Mrs Latimer had departed about her own affairs, and he was alone in the house. He wandered round aimlessly, lifting an ornament here, an article there, turning on the television and turning it off again, uninterested in ordinary pursuits. He had never before realised exactly how empty a house could seem, and he wondered with unusual insight whether that was how Helen felt when he was away.

But that was different, he thought savagely. And that was what she had wanted anyway. She had proved it now by walking out on him.

Eventually, he took a bottle of Scotch up to his bedroom and it was morning before he tried to use his tired brain again. . .

Helen let herself into the house in Kersland Square not without some misgivings. But she had known that sooner or later she must come and as it was almost a week since Jake was due to leave for Tsaba she felt reasonably safe.

Mrs Howard had not wanted her to leave. After their initial antipathy with one another, a genuine respect and liking had grown up between them, and Helen had begun to realise that Jake's mother was sorry she wanted a divorce.

In the early days they had talked quite a lot about Jake's early life and Helen had been given an insight into her husband's character. His mother was intensely proud of him, but she had never changed, and because of this deep down Jake had not changed either. He was still just as scornful of artifice as he had ever been, although he used the very system he despised to his own ends.

Helen had learned about his father, and the way they had had to skimp themselves to send Jake to university, and she began to realise why Jake thought so little of the county set who had always had everything laid on for them.

But in spite of that, he had been lucky. He had happened to be in the right place at the right time, and his excellent brain had served him well. He had succeeded when others had failed because he had a single-minded approach to life, allowing nothing and no one to get in his way.

Only occasionally Mrs Howard had mentioned the women in Jake's life. She had told Helen about Veronica Quarton, and of the way she had thrown herself at his head. The Quartons still lived in the town; Mr Quarton was retired now, while his wife continued her spate of affairs with younger men.

All these things had moulded Jake's character; had moulded his opinion of women; had taught him to take what was offered and never to offer anything in return.

But within the last couple of days Mrs Howard's questions had become more personal. She had been trying to find the real reason why Helen had suddenly decided she wanted to leave Jake, but Helen could not divulge that, even to her. So she had quietly, but firmly, made arrangements to leave, and Mrs Howard had not tried to stop her.

Now Helen closed the front door silently. The last thing she wanted was to run into Mrs Latimer before she had had chance to pack her things. She could not stand a lot of questions from her. For the present she intended to book herself anonymously into a small hotel and then she could set about looking for a flat or an apartment in earnest.

She climbed the stairs quietly. In a cream trouser suit and low-heeled shoes she made no sound on the soft carpet of the stairway, but at the top of the flight she halted hesitantly outside Jake's door. The desire to see his room one last time impelled her to open the door, but when she did so she fell back aghast.

The room was in chaos, clothes strewn carelessly across the floor, and draped haphazardly over the backs of chairs and dressing table. The curtains were drawn even at this late hour of the morning, and a stale odour of cigar smoke and Scotch invaded her nostrils.

Shaking her head incredulously, she took a step into the room and as she did so a harsh voice called savagely: 'Get out! I've told you, Mrs Latimer, damn you! *Get out*!'

Helen was horrified. Pressing a hand to her throat, she stepped further into the room and now she could see that the bed she had thought just rumpled, the covers dragged roughly across it, was occupied. Jake lay among the crumpled sheets, the growth of several days' beard upon his chin, his eyes closed against the band of light the opened door admitted.

'*Get out*!' he muttered again, resting an arm across his eyes and opening them slowly. 'I said—' Then he halted abruptly, as he saw Helen, his eyes narrowing disbelievingly. 'Oh, God!' she heard him mutter faintly. 'God! I'm seeing things!'

Helen hesitated only a moment and then she took the few steps to the bed, looking down on him incomprehensibly. 'You're not seeing things, Jake,' she said quietly. Then, more forcefully: 'For heaven's sake, how long have you been like this?'

Her eyes took in the empty Scotch bottles beside the bed, the dirty glasses tumbled on the bedside table. Then she looked back at him, a look of compassion in her green eyes.

Jake opened his eyes again, and heaving a sigh, rolled over on to his stomach, taking the covers with him. He was naked from the waist up, his lower limbs wrapped in the silk sheets.

'Go away, Helen,' he muttered violently. 'Go away. I don't want to see anyone. Get out of my room! You don't live here any more, remember?'

Helen hesitated only a moment, and then with a determined gesture she took off her suit jacket and threw it over a nearby chair. She went to the windows first and drawing back the curtains she allowed the watery November sun to invade the room. She thrust open the lower windows, and a chill northerly breeze blew in, dispersing the stale air.

Then she turned back to Jake, who was burying his head under the pillow. 'I said get out of here!' he repeated angrily. 'I don't need your pity!'

'You haven't got it!' retorted Helen, with feeling. 'Good lord, Jake, you must have been on quite a trip!'

Jake rolled on to his back and shaded his eyes. 'Shut those curtains, and get out of here!'

'No.'

Helen ignored him and continued picking up his crumpled garments from the floor. She threw them all out on to the landing, mentally noting that she must ask Mrs Latimer to deal with them all. Then she came to the bed.

'Get up!' she said, looking down at him, her hands on her hips. 'I'm going to make the bed.'

'Like hell you are!' Jake struggled into a sitting position, and now she could see the lines of strain and weariness about his face. 'Helen, answer me one thing! What are you doing here?'

Helen shrugged her shoulders. 'I—I came to get my things,' she answered honestly. 'I thought you'd be in Tsaba by now.'

'Where have you been?' Jake stared at her grimly.

'Actually, I've been in Yorkshire.' she said. 'Selby, to be precise. Now, are you going to get up?'

Jake was staring at her disbelievingly. 'You're not trying to tell me you've been with my mother all this time?'

'I am. But I don't intend to discuss it right now.' Helen turned deliberately to the door, picking up her coat as she went. 'I'll be downstairs if you want me.'

'Helen!' His tone was tortured. 'You—you won't disappear again?'

Helen halted by the door, her face suffusing with colour at the look in his eyes. 'Not until you're dressed anyway,' she promised lightly, more lightly than she felt, and went downstairs.

In the lounge she pressed the palms of her trembling hands against her hot cheeks. A wild presentiment of excitement was flooding her being and she couldn't sit still.

She walked restlessly about the room and started when a sound behind her brought her swinging round to face Mrs Latimer.

'Mrs Howard!' she exclaimed weakly. 'Oh, Mrs Howard, am I glad to see you!'

Helen smiled. 'Are you, Mrs Latimer?'

'Oh, yes, madam, yes!' Mrs Latimer stared at her as though she couldn't believe her eyes. 'Mr Jake has been nearly out of his mind with worry.' She pressed a hand to her throat. 'We—Tom and I—we've not been able to get near him. He's been up in his room for days, eating nothing, taking no calls, just drinking himself into unconsciousness. Oh, you've no idea what it's been like, Mrs Howard! I nearly contacted his mother, but he swore he'd dismiss us both if we tried to interfere.'

Helen went across to her kindly. 'How terrible for you,' she said gently, and to her dismay Mrs Latimer burst into tears.

'I'm sorry, Mrs Howard,' she sobbed, 'but I think the world of Mr Jake, and seeing him there, so morose and depressed, killing himself with that filthy stuff—'

'All right, Mrs Latimer.' Helen bit her lip, moved by the housekeeper's emotions. 'Go on now, stop worrying. You can make us both some tea.'

'Us, madam? For you—and—and—'

'Me!' remarked a voice behind them, and they both looked towards the door in surprise. Jake was leaning against the jamb, water sparkling on his hair indicating that he had just had a shower. He had shaved too, and endeavoured to smooth his hair, which Helen noticed inconsequently needed cutting. But he had not dressed; he was wearing a white towelling bathrobe that reached his knees and tied with a sash of the same material.

'Oh, sir!' Mrs Latimer's voice trembled.

'Go and make the tea!' advised Jake quietly, and Mrs Latimer scurried past him like an obedient rabbit.

Helen for her part felt suddenly nervous. It had seemed so easy, thinking of what she would say when he came down. But now that he was here, she was speechless.

Jake moved into the room, and stood looking about him thoughtfully. Then he bent and extracted a cheroot from the box on the low table and lit it with the heavy carved table lighter. When he straightened, his eyes flickered to Helen, and he said in a low compelling tone: 'Why didn't you tell me where you'd gone?'

Helen moved awkwardly. 'I—er—I didn't want you to find me. I thought if I could keep out of your way until you'd left for Tsaba—'

'But why?' His voice had hardened, and a muscle jerked near his jawline. 'Were you so frightened of me?'

Helen bent her head. 'How—how long have you been—drinking?' she asked softly, changing the subject abruptly.

Jake flung himself carelessly into a chair, his eyes hard. 'Does it matter?'

'What do you mean?'

'What I say.' Jake heaved a sigh and looked down at the glowing tip of his cheroot. 'Look, Helen, I've been thinking while I was in the shower. Upstairs—well, I guess I was—shocked to see you. But now the initial stage is over and I'm wondering exactly why you're hanging about here. I mean—okay—you came for your things. But don't let my condition worry you. I'm perfectly all right, as you can see—'

'You're not all right!' Helen burst out hotly. 'You know you're not. Mrs Latimer—'

'Oh, Mrs Latimer!' Jake was scathing. 'Mrs Latimer is an old woman. She doesn't understand.'

'I think she understands very well!' exclaimed Helen tremulously, her earlier excitement giving way to a kind of aching dread.

'You're entitled to your opinion, of course.' Jake tapped ash carelessly into the polished hearth.

'Jake!' Helen's cry was a mixture of pain and exasperation. 'Please! Stop talking like that.'

'Why?' Jake's eyes narrowed. 'How do you expect me to behave, Helen? Sneaking back here like a thief in the night!'

'It wasn't like that—'

'Then why did you go to my mother's answer me that?' His lips twisted. 'Oh, don't bother, I know. You went there because you knew I hadn't a cat in hell's chance of finding you. The very last place I'd look would be my own backyard, and you knew that, damn you!'

Helen sighed. 'Well, what if I did?' She shook her head. 'Your mother was very kind.'

'I'll bet she was!' Jake chewed moodily at the cheroot. 'And what did you tell her? What excuse did you give for running away?'

'I didn't give any excuse. I told her I wanted a divorce.'

'Like hell you did!' Jake sprang up out of his chair. 'And what about me? Don't I get consulted, is that it? You planned to arrange all the details while I was out of the country?'

Put like that it sounded so cold, so calculating, and Helen could do nothing but stand there silently and allow the wave of his anger to sweep over her.

Jake threw the remains of the cheroot into the grate, walking abruptly over to the cocktail cabinet, but Helen was there before him, blocking his access.

'No,' she said urgently, grasping his forearms. 'Please, Jake, listen to me!'

Jake looked down at her slim hands gripping the white material of his bathrobe. 'I've listened to you long enough, Helen,' he muttered, a trifle thickly. 'First you tell Jennifer you're leaving me, and then my own mother! How much do you think I can take?'

'But, Jake, I thought it was the best way—' she murmured, aware of the hard muscular strength of his arm beneath her fingers.

'Why?' he demanded savagely. 'Because of my behaviour?'

'No, because of mine!' cried Helen piteously.

Jake stared down into her pale face with tormented eyes. 'Say that again,' he commanded huskily.

'What?' Helen shook her head wearily.

'That bit about your behaviour! What in hell are you talking about?' His eyes darkened. 'Are you involved with Mannering after all?'

Helen's lips parted. 'You know I'm not!' she exclaimed.

Jake released himself from her and raked a confused hand through his hair. 'Then for God's sake, what are you talking about?'

Helen wet her dry lips with her tongue. 'That— that night,' she whispered unhappily. 'When—

when you came to my room.'

Jake's lashes veiled his eyes. 'You mean here—in this house?'

'Of course.' Helen was tremulous. 'Oh, Jake, you must know what happened!'

Jake frowned. 'Yes, I know,' he said heavily. 'I let you down.'

Helen lifted her shoulders. 'You could say that,' she murmured, her cheeks burning with remembered humiliation.

Jake ran a hand round the back of his neck impatiently. 'But, Helen,' he muttered violently, 'I'm a man, not a saint! You asked the impossible!'

Helen looked up into his dark eyes, pain burning deep in hers. 'Did I?' she asked huskily. 'Then it's all over, isn't it?'

Jake uttered an exclamation. 'Does it have to be?' he demanded insistently. 'Helen, I know I'm beyond contempt, but if it's any consolation to you, my only excuse is that I love you, and I've never said that to any woman!'

Helen stared at him incredulously. 'You—love—me?' she breathed weakly.

Jake stared at her for a long moment and then something in his control snapped and he reached for her savagely, crushing her up against him, finding her willing mouth with his, kissing her with all the pent-up agony of these last days without her.

And Helen returned his kisses eagerly, clinging to him when he would have lifted his head, drowning in the sensuality he aroused inside her. Her body was moulded to his, her arms round his waist, clinging to him with an abandon that dispelled for all time his doubts that she was not a warm and passionate woman.

When he finally lifted his head, his face was pale, and there was an agonised glitter in his eyes. 'What do you think you're doing to me?' he muttered hoarsely. 'God, Helen, if you don't want to take the consequences, then you'd better get out of here pretty damn quick!'

Helen continued to gaze at him adoringly, her fingers at his waist, caressing his hips. 'You're not going to get rid of me that easily,' she whispered, touching her lips to the corner of his mouth.

Jake stared at her, a haunted look in his eyes. 'You don't want to go? Helen, don't play games with me!'

'I'm not playing games, darling, I love you,' she breathed, stroking the dark sideburns on his cheeks. 'It's all been a terrible mistake. I thought you—had rejected me!'

'That night in your room?' Jake pulled her to him, unable to prevent the urgency of his need to hold her. 'Helen, if only you'd known how I felt that night. I blamed myself, you see, for that nightmare. I despised myself utterly for taking advantage of you, for forcing myself on you.'

'But the morning after you were so cold,' she began.

Jake half smiled now. 'Wouldn't anyone have been? God, I thought—now you've really done it! I wanted to get down on my knees and tell you I was sorry, that I wouldn't let it happen again, and you just kept on saying it wasn't important, and it drove me mad!' He buried his face in the hair on her neck. 'Helen, these last days have been absolute hell! I couldn't eat, I couldn't sleep! I thought I'd lost everything!'

Helen pressed her face to his chest. 'When I came here today and found you like that, I thought it might be so. I prayed it was. But then you came downstairs so coldly, indifferently, I wanted to die!'

Jake shook his head. 'You don't know me yet, Helen. I have to hide my feelings. I'm afraid I couldn't have stood your pity. When you appeared in my bedroom just now I was convinced I was having hallucinations!'

'Oh, Jake.' Helen felt an overwhelming sense of protectiveness assail her. 'What fools we've been!'

'Yes, but no longer.' Jake put her determinedly away from him, fastening the cord of his bathrobe. 'Now, I'll go and get dressed and take you out to lunch at the most expensive restaurant in town!'

Helen tilted her head. 'I'd rather you didn't,' she murmured softly. 'I don't want to share you with a lot of other people. Couldn't we just have lunch here?'

Jake's eyes darkened. 'If that's what you want?'

'Oh, yes, please.' Helen nodded. Then she turned away, bending her head suddenly. 'Jake— this trip to Tsaba—'

Jake caught her close to him, pressing her back against him. 'There'll be no more trips,' he replied huskily. 'Or at least if there are, you'll be along. How does Central Africa strike you as a honeymoon spot?' His mouth lingered disturbingly against her neck.

Helen took a shaky breath. 'We've had our honeymoon,' she murmured doubtfully.

'Oh, no, we haven't,' retorted Jake, his hands sliding possessively over her. 'But we will, my darling, we will. . .'

For the spirited lover
in you...

Presents...™

Passionate, compelling,
provocative romances
you'll never want to end.

Eight brand new titles
each month

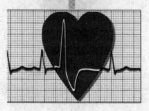